Taking Risk in Summit County

Taking Risk in Summit County

Summit County Series, Book 4

Katherine Karrol

Contents

Chapter 1

Okay, this is it – the last run for today and could be the last one of your life. Make it count.

Clay Cooper took one more long look down the slope and took in the scene, in case it was his last chance. He studied the view below from his vantage point atop Titan, the highest run on Summit Mountain, and took in a deep, cold breath. The snowy landscape below mesmerized him, thanks to the four inches of snow that had fallen overnight and covered the pine forest that stretched out for miles. It also helped that his more immediate view was not cluttered with people. The best part of making his own work schedule and being friends with a ski instructor was that he could come out for some early-morning weekday skiing before the rest of Summit County even finished their morning coffee. He turned to his brother Derek and friend Trig and grinned.

"See you down there."

He shoved off and crouched down to pick up speed as he approached the moguls. He loved the feel of the cold air on his face and the hard earth under his feet. The fresh coating of snow made the terrain slightly harder to see, but he knew these hills and moguls like the back of his hand. He also liked a challenge – and risk.

As he reached the bottom of the hill, he laughed. *No snap or pain. I win.*

He turned back and looked up at the hill. "Better luck next time, Titan."

By the time the hills started to fill up, Clay and Derek had said goodbye to Trig and were heading home to shower and go to work.

"This will be our last early ski for a while, brother. I'm glad you were able to come out this morning, before everything changes."

"You make it sound like I'm moving to Mars or something. I'll still come out to ski before work sometimes."

Clay laughed and gave his brother a sarcastic look. "Yeah, right. After waiting and hoping and praying for years for the chance to marry Rachel, do you really think you're going to want to leave her in the mornings to come and ski?"

Derek grinned and blushed a bit as he was probably imagining waking up next to her. "No, probably not for a while."

Clay laughed. "Definitely not. Like I said, everything is changing. It's a good change though. It's long overdue and I'm happy for you. You've got everything you want now."

He ignored the stab in his gut as he said it.

He was truly happy for his younger brother. The whole family had felt the loss when he and Rachel had broken up almost four years before, and they were all thrilled when they had reunited and quickly gotten re-engaged at Christmas.

It was just that seeing others get what *he* wanted hit Clay's competitive nerve and reminded him that he was three years behind on his own wedding plans – life plans, really. Even though life had taken turns he hadn't anticipated over the last several years, he still hadn't gotten used to not having things go the way he planned – in other words, *losing.*

They broke down what needed to be done at the family insurance agency while Derek was on his honeymoon as they made their way over the rolling hills and around the gentle curves of the two-lane highways that led home to Hideaway. It looked as if God Himself had personally painted the snow, heavily on the thick branches of the tall pines and lightly on the trunks of the other trees, and Derek took pictures along the way, hoping to use them for a future painting of his own.

Derek listed out what would need to be addressed and what could wait. "I've been trying to get everything in place so that you don't have to do the stuff you hate any more than necessary."

"Thanks, but you know you don't have to do that. I did it before we restructured everything and separated our jobs, and I can do it again for a week. That being said, I do appreciate the time you've put in so that I don't have to do what I hate."

"Just remember that someday when you're planning *your* honeymoon and setting up sales calls."

"Don't worry, I'm not going on a honeymoon anytime soon." He let out a laugh. "I'm also not giving you any of my sales."

"You could have a honeymoon sooner if you stopped being so picky and gave up your two-year Love Plan." Derek loved to rip on Clay for writing off women quickly if they didn't click and his plan to date for a year, be engaged for a year, then marry, and took every opportunity to do so.

"You mean my solid, smart, reasonable plan? I'm not giving that one up. And I'm not picky, I just know what I want."

"Whatever." Derek chuckled and returned to the subject at hand. "It's still weird to think about how different things are at work. You really saved the agency, along with our sanity and our family, with the plan you came up with to get dad on board with restructuring. Now *that* was a solid, smart, reasonable plan."

"Oh, come on. *That* plan came out of the conversations you and I had about everything we hated about our jobs and the agency."

"Clayton, stop being humble. You organized it all *and* sold Dad on it – that was nothing short of miraculous. The fact that I didn't move away from here to start over and don't dread going into the office every day is testament to the plan you put into motion. I shudder to think what would have happened if you hadn't convinced Dad to make changes. I might have moved away without clearing the air with Rachel and I might not be three days away from marrying the love of my life."

"I'm glad you stayed, but it was a family effort that turned things around. Dad's heart attack convinced him more than I ever could have and cleared the way for all of the changes that needed to be made. The more I think about it, the more I think things had to get to the breaking point the way they did in order for change to happen. It's just like when I got so miserable and ready to walk out of there. If I hadn't gotten to the misery, I wouldn't have looked for a different way to do things."

Clay had his turn at being miserable and considering other jobs a few years back and at that time he had decided that he needed to either leave it or find something to love there and do it well. He decided to find a way to make the job his own and to give it everything he had for two years. If at the end of that time he was still miserable, he would leave.

He became obsessed with learning everything he could about sales and customer service and put it into practice. It was like every other project he'd taken on and he found a way to make it work. He found that he loved and excelled at it and that it gave him the challenge he had always craved.

The problem was that he hated the rest of the tasks involved with running the business. Since the restructuring, they all focused on the parts they were best at and worked together as a team; so far the system was working beautifully.

"Just promise me one, thing, Derek. When you leave work tomorrow for the last time as a single man, leave every thought of work there. Focus on your big day and your big future. We've got everything under control and you deserve the chance to enjoy yourself. It was a long time coming."

"Thanks. And now that I'm getting married and the business is going well, you can get back to your life."

"What does that mean?"

"Come on, Clay. You practically put your life on hold for the past few years because of family things. You did so much for me when I was so depressed, and when the agency started tanking, you hit the pavement to make sales to keep it going to lighten the load on Dad. You missed your deadline for getting married and we all know how you love your plans. It's your turn now – you deserve to be happy, too."

"Are you trying to big brother me, little brother?"

"You know I'm right."

Chapter 2

C lay pinned the boutonniere to Derek's lapel and was straightening the shoulders of his tuxedo when their parents came into the small Sunday School room where they were getting ready.

His mother's eyes misted up as soon as she saw Derek in his tux. "You look so handsome. Just wait until you see your bride. She's a vision."

His father smiled at him. "Your mother is right, and Rachel's smile is as big as yours. I think we're ready to get this show on the road, but we wanted to come back and pray with you before it all starts."

They shared their last prayer as a family of four and their father prayed for the wedding that was about to start as well as for both of his sons' marriages and the future generations of the family.

∞∞∞

Clay took his place next to Derek in the front of the old church after escorting his parents to their seat. "This is what you've been waiting for. Congratulations." He grinned at him and patted him on the shoulder as the processional music started.

As he watched the bridesmaids, Brianna Callahan and Shelby Montaugh, glide down the aisle, he was struck by how elegant they looked. *When did they turn into women? I guess that's what happens when you don't see someone for a while.*

They had both been away at college for some time, and since Derek and Rachel had been broken up, they didn't all run in the same circles any more. As much as he tried, he couldn't take his eyes off of one of them.

When their eyes met, his heart skipped a beat and he felt a shock wave down to his toes. He quickly chastised himself for having such a reaction to a young girl. When it hit him that she was a grown woman and not a child, it didn't make him feel any less guilty. There were multiple reasons not to allow himself to think about her, and he reminded himself that he didn't waste time looking at women who were off-limits.

He redirected his eyes to the bride, who had just come into view flanked by her parents. He looked over at Derek and it was as if his brother was seeing a glimpse of heaven itself. Clay smiled and prayed for the marriage he was about to witness as everyone stood.

He always got bored during weddings and his mind always wandered, so he focused his eyes on Pastor Ray, waiting for his cue to hand over the ring. When he did so, he knew he was home free and his mind could wander all it wanted without messing anything up.

When it started to wander back to the bridesmaid, he chastised himself again for being out of line and forced himself to think about the X Games he'd watched earlier in the day. *You really need to start dating if you're looking at your new sister-in-law's best friend. Not cool, man.*

Before long he was thinking about her again, but this time he thought back to the last real conversation he'd had with her a few years before, when she had given him a much-needed butt-kicking while a group of them were cross country skiing at Marvel Point.

"Why haven't you joined us at Summit Mountain, Clay?"

"You apparently missed the news about my career-ending knee injury."

"I don't think anyone in town missed *that* news. You look like you're getting around well. Are you still having a problem with it?"

"Not really, but now that I've torn my ACL twice, I have to be careful."

"You? Careful? Last time we were both rehabbing knee injuries, you couldn't wait to get out and try it again. I know this one was bad, but chances are you're not going to get plowed into on the slopes, and you can control how much challenge you're giving it. You look completely bored out here, and I'm guessing you would rather be racing down a mountain right now than across a beach."

"I would give anything to be racing down a mountain right now. I just don't think I should be taking the risk of an injury that would end any chance of skiing or anything else fun."

"It seems like you're taking the risk now of being bored to death by playing it safe and not doing what you love. That's not really you. Why don't you come snowboarding with us? It would be easier on your knee, but you would be on the Mountain."

Just then their conversation got interrupted by Derek throwing a snowball at him. After winning the snowball fight and racing her back to the cars, Clay thought about what she had said. It gave him the push he needed to take risks again and see what happened. Of all the people in his life, she was the only one who had challenged him to start living again.

He did start snowboarding, and when he remained injury-free and got his confidence in his knee back up, he started skiing again. When he did that for a while, he got his devil-may-care attitude back, tackled Titan again, and felt like himself for the first time in months.

He owed her a great debt of gratitude. *And now you're staring at her again. Knock it off.*

The reception wasn't much better. Since the wedding party was seated together, there was no way to create much distance between himself and her. The toast the two bridesmaids gave had everyone alternately laughing and dabbing their eyes. He wondered if they had planned for Shelby to tell the stories and Brianna to interrupt to add details or corrections, or if they just couldn't help acting normally. Either way, it was endearing and touched Rachel and Derek. It also showed his own toast up.

"Thanks a lot, ladies. What's with upstaging me? Don't you know it's tradition for the best man's toast to be the best one?"

They both giggled as they looked at each other, then at him. Shelby nudged him. "Clay, only you would turn a wedding toast into a competition."

Brianna almost spit out the drink she had just taken a sip of and turned to Shelby. "Hello, kettle? This is pot. You're black."

They all shared plenty of laughs and stories during dinner, and Clay shared the obligatory dance with each of them. He chastised himself for enjoying one of the dances more than he should and wishing the song was longer.

Suddenly in the middle of the evening, she was gone. He was both relieved and disappointed when she wasn't there to take all of his attention away from the rest of the crowd.

Chapter 3

Two weeks later, Clay straightened his tie and practiced his "I'm so happy for you and don't think it's at all weird that you're getting married after being back together for two weeks" smile. *Another day, another wedding, after another short engagement. What is it with the people in this town lately?*

Truth be told, it was easy to be as happy for Rick and Faith, the day's bride and groom and Rachel's parents, as it had been for Derek and Rachel two weeks before. They had been apart for years and had never gotten over each other, and he had seen how cozy and happy they looked together at Derek and Rachel's reception.

He arrived at the church just as Joe Callahan and Emily Spencer, yet another couple who had recently gotten engaged after a short courtship, were getting out of Joe's car. He'd been good friends with Joe for most of his life and Emily had moved to town at the end of the summer. Joe had lost his first wife suddenly a few years before and was left to care for a newborn while grieving, and it was great to see his old friend happy again.

"This will be you two soon. Congratulations again." He shook Joe's hand and hugged Emily.

"Thanks, Clay. We thought *we* were going to have a short engagement with our wedding being a couple of months out, but this one has to be some kind of record. I guess when you know, you know, right?"

He smiled. "Right." *What does that even mean? And how can you know that she is who she says she is after such a short time?* He liked Emily and she seemed genuine, but he'd learned from experience that people were not always what they seemed and that sometimes it took a long time for the truth to reveal itself.

Even before having bad experiences, Clay had never understood whirlwind romances. It made no sense to him to jump into something so important without careful consideration. To him it made sense to date for a year and have a year engagement, and he was sticking with his plan.

Since he had also planned to be married by the time he was twenty-eight and he was staring down the barrel at his twenty-ninth birthday, he was, by his count, three years behind. He had also planned to be married for two years before having children, so fatherhood was getting pushed back, too. The only things that were on track according to the timeline he had set for himself were his career and home ownership. They were important and he had wanted them in place before marriage, but they didn't keep him warm at night.

He walked up the stairs to the sanctuary in the old church where Derek was acting as usher. As son-in-law to both the bride and groom, he was taking his duties very seriously.

"Hey, brother. Does it feel weird being back here for another wedding so soon?"

"Not as weird as ushering for a wedding for two people who hated each other a month ago. Who knows, maybe you'll be next and I'll be standing in a church ushering people to watch you do this. I highly recommend it, by the way." He grinned as he offered Clay his arm to walk him down the aisle.

Clay laughed and hit his arm as he followed him down the short aisle to the pew where their parents were already seated. He looked around the sparsely populated church and nodded greetings to the few people in attendance. The bride and groom wanted a wedding that was quick and small, so he knew everyone in the room except for a handful of people who came up from Chicago and Grand Rapids for the groom.

As far as he could tell, Shelby and Brianna would be the only two single women at this one, and he reminded himself that they didn't count. He had worked hard to shove the thoughts that he'd had a couple of weeks before out of his mind and avoided looking in their direction just in case.

She's off limits and doesn't count; she might as well be a guy.

Clay had never had a hard time getting women. He always had dates and girlfriends when he wanted them – and wasn't too busy for them – in college, and had a couple of relationships that had lasted for several months. He was considering proposing to the second one, but when he was vulnerable and needed her the most, she was gone. That only solidified his commitment to his two-year plan.

When he returned to Hideaway, his small northern Michigan hometown, after graduation, he found that the dating pool went from Olympic-sized to backyard kiddie. Work took him to Traverse City regularly, so he still had opportunities to meet women, but he just hadn't met any that he wanted to go out with more than a few times. People had encouraged him to try a dating app, but he wasn't ready to jump into that cesspool quite yet.

> *Looking for: normal, sane, honest woman who loves Jesus, family, and fun. Must enjoy various seasonal outdoor activities and be willing to live in a tiny town on the sandy shores of Lake Michigan.*
>
> *Multiple references required.*

The ceremony was short, his favorite kind. It was great that they'd found each other again after many years apart, and they seemed made for each other. While it would be nice to have someone to reunite with like that and have a shorter timeline with,

Clay was thankful for the fact that he'd never had to go through losing the love of his life in the first place. It was one benefit of never having had one.

He saw the way Rick, the groom, looked at Faith, the bride. It was the same way Derek looked at Rachel. It was a look of pure adoration, one that he had never worn. He'd seen it on the faces of women he'd known and dated in college, but their adoration was more for his status as football hero than for him as a person.

Glancing over at his parents, he saw the same looks on their faces. He'd seen that look many times over the past three months since they had almost lost his dad, and it warmed his heart.

Someday. Maybe.

He headed toward the back door of the church while everyone congratulated the bride and groom so that he could walk the few short blocks to Evelyn Glover's house, the Shoreside Inn, where the celebration dinner would commence. He was looking forward to seeing the renovations Joe and Emily had been working so hard on in the beautiful Victorian home over the past few months. Knowing how talented Joe was, he expected it to be something to behold.

He had volunteered to help with getting the food set up and was looking forward to a little power walk to get some cold, fresh air and get his heart pumping first. As he turned the corner, he saw Shelby sitting on the bench by the door.

She looked up and smiled. "Hi, Clay. Did you happen to see Brianna making her way down here? She's my ride."

Shelby looked exhausted. He had heard that the chronic illness she had been battling for the last few years could really take her down, but it was unsettling to see the girl who used to be involved in every sport available look so tired and weak.

"Why don't you ride over with me? Text Brianna and tell her you found a better offer while I bring the car around." He smiled as he headed through the door without giving her a chance to say no.

The chill in the air felt good on his face as he walked to his car. He didn't mind exchanging his planned walk to help Shelby out. There was never a bad time to help a friend in need, and he had seen Brianna in deep conversation with Rick's sister upstairs.

She got into the car quickly, rubbing her hands together against the early March chill. "Thanks, Clay. I was hoping to get home and get everything set before Aunt Evelyn gets there."

"Me too. I'll need some direction, but I'm sure you can show me what to do." Shelby had been living with her aunt for the past couple of months since graduating from college and would know where everything was and needed to go.

"There isn't much to do. Aunt Evelyn and Emily have preparing for parties down to a science, so the setup won't take long at all." She stifled a yawn.

Clay laughed. "I think we should start with the coffee."

"Good plan."

When they arrived at the house, Emily and Joe were there and were almost finished getting things set up. Emily had been living in the house since she'd moved to town as well, and it was obvious that she had a handle on what went where.

Shelby started to go into the dining room to help, but Emily took one look at her and suggested she go rest upstairs. Shelby started to protest, then got caught up in another yawn. "Maybe just for a few minutes. Will you ask Brianna or Rachel to wake me up before we eat if I fall asleep?"

"Sure." He watched her walk up the stairs slowly and with what looked like a lot of discomfort and he pictured her running on the track back in high school. She trained with the varsity track team when she was a freshman and he was a senior, and she kept up with and often passed by the varsity girls effortlessly. They ran with a local group when he was in college, too, as did Derek, Rachel, and Brianna, and she was usually in the lead. He wondered why the competitive girl he had known didn't seem to push through whatever was going on the way she'd pushed through sports injuries, or the way he had.

Joe gave him a quick tour of the projects they had finished on the downstairs level, and the place looked amazing. Between their handiwork and Evelyn's decorating flair, the place looked as if it was restored to its original grandeur.

When the guests started to arrive, Clay helped with taking coats and directing people into the parlor, then set out to make sure everyone had something to drink. When he introduced himself to Rick's friend Tim, who had driven up from Chicago for the wedding, he heard the familiar note of recognition in his voice.

"Clay Cooper, the quarterback? I lost a big bet on that Orange Bowl."

Clay gave his standard smile and response. "How much do I owe you?"

Tim chuckled as he put his hands up in apology. "Sorry, you've probably heard that more than you would like. I felt your pain when you went down with that blown knee. I had the same thing happen in college, although I wasn't being talked about as a first-round draft pick like you were."

"Life can change in the blink of an eye. Fortunately, my knee holds up pretty well now that pass rushers aren't gunning for me."

"Same here. Life does have its crazy turns – just look at the wedding we're here for as proof."

Clay smiled. "That's for sure, but God works everything for good, right?"

"Right. I can sure see why you would return to your hometown after all of that. This place is straight out of a postcard."

"It is. It's a great little community, and Rick is a good addition to it. Speaking of that, I'm supposed to be helping out here and if you'll excuse me, I'm going to go see if I can be useful in the kitchen."

He walked into the kitchen, and seeing that everything looked set in there, he continued out through the back door for a bit of fresh air. It had been several months since he'd been recognized, and even though it happened less and less frequently, he always hoped each time would be the last. He had relived that injury a thousand times in his head, and it never got any easier. Life *did* change in the blink of an eye.

He did what he always did when he got those reminders. *Lord, You used that injury to save me from going further down the bad road I was on and I thank You for it. Even though part of me still wishes it never happened, I thank You for it.*

"Clay! What are you doing out here? You scared me half to death." Brianna grabbed onto the porch railing to avoid falling right into him.

He reached out and stabilized her on the step, careful of where he put his hands. "Sorry about that. I just came out for some fresh air."

"Can you hand me some of those pops? We're running a little low in there."

"Sure." He handed some to her, loaded his own arms up, and followed her back into the kitchen.

She pulled a Vernors out of the pile. "I'm going to take this up to Shelby."

"Is she sick? I mean, other than the usual."

Brianna gave him a look. "She's been horribly sick for five years, Clay. Sick *is* the usual." With that, she sighed and walked out of the room.

I feel sorry for the guy who ends up with that *one.*

He reminded himself that Brianna saved her wrath for people who hurt the downtrodden and shook it off. She was a good friend to Shelby in her time of need, just like she had been a good friend to Rachel in hers. Some day she would probably be president or ruler of the world.

He thought back to the story Brianna and Shelby had told at Derek and Rachel's wedding about conspiring to get Rachel to send a DNA swab into a genealogy database under the guise of gaining some genetic information about her unknown father, all the while secretly hoping that they would find him. Brianna had even let Rick think she was the child he'd been matched with to check him out and make sure he was legit before even telling Rachel about his existence.

He chuckled as he pictured Brianna and Shelby grilling Rick on a conference call before agreeing to tell Rachel about him. If not for the two of them, Rachel would still not have a father and the wedding they had just attended would not have happened.

When they descended the stairs a few minutes later, he had to avert his eyes again. *Seriously, man, stop it; you're being out of line again. Maybe you* should *try online dating.*

When Clay got home, he was hoping he would be able to go straight to sleep instead of having to rehash every play of the drive that took him down and took away his NFL dreams. He might have had a chance if two other people hadn't mentioned watching his career implode at the reception.

He still kicked himself for allowing the injury to happen – for actually *causing* it – and he still blamed himself for the loss. He knew he was about to get tackled, but was determined to get the needed first down. Instead of sliding and avoiding the hit, he ran for the extra yard and got slammed to the ground, his knee twisting as he went.

Since it wasn't his first ACL tear, he knew what had happened the moment he felt the familiar pain. He also knew that it was worse than the one the year before and that his planned NFL career was gone in that instant. The announcer and analyst had immediately predicted that a second ACL tear would get him labeled injury-prone, and potentially reckless, and take him off every team's draft board, and they were right. Instead of being drafted high in the first round as anticipated before the injury, he was passed on by every team through every round. The draft was more excruciating than the injury could ever be.

When the Forty-Niners called him a week later and signed him as an undrafted free agent, he thought he had another chance, but when the knee didn't heal as well or as quickly as it should have as the season approached, they cut him. They were impressed enough with his knowledge and understanding of the game to offer him a job as an assistant to an assistant coach, but he decided that being on the sidelines without being a player would be too painful a reminder of all he had lost. He returned to his hometown with his tail between his legs and learned the family insurance business.

Once he started getting over the anger at how his future had gone up in smoke, and how he was to blame, he took a long, hard look at how he had been living and who he had started to become and knew that the injury was a life-saving gift. It probably would have been hard for anyone in his position to resist the lure of the spotlight, the accolades, and the hero mantle, and it would have been hard for any man to resist the lure of beautiful women who would do anything to be seen on his arm, but he had known better and should have done better.

He knew that God had forgiven him for falling to temptations, but he hadn't quite figured out how to forgive himself, or if he should. Instead, he did what he could to avoid all of those temptations; he kept his distance with the women he dated, and he deflected compliments and avoided spotlights as much as possible.

Chapter 4

C lay drove slowly on the icy street as he and his mother made their way to the Bay Shore Diner. They had started the tradition of having breakfast together when he was in college and didn't get home much. It was her way of getting some alone time with her son during a weekend that was always filled with activities and friends. After he moved back to Hideaway, it turned into a monthly event that they both looked forward to.

He wasn't surprised to find the parking lot nearly empty. "Bunch of amateurs think they need to stay home just because of a little ice. What's happening to the people in this town?"

Carol laughed. "Be nice, Clayton. You're going to wish more people stayed home when we're here in July and have to wait in line."

After they gave their orders, Clay looked at his mother. "You're unusually quiet today, Mom. Is everything okay? Is Dad okay?"

"Everything is fine, I've just been doing a lot of thinking and praying about you lately. I've been watching you, especially at the recent weddings."

Clay felt the heat rise in his cheeks. *Oh, geez, I hope she didn't see me staring at a certain bridesmaid.*

"You know, it may be time for some changes for you."

"What do you mean?"

"Well, you've been focusing on everything but your own life for the last few years. Between what Derek went through and the tough time the business went through and the effect it had on your dad, and how *I* reacted to your dad, you carried a lot on your shoulders. You became the family caretaker to some degree, and while you did a great job, it's over now. I've wondered for a while if part of the reason you were so willing to focus on what the family needed was because it gave you an excuse to stay out of relationships. Now there really isn't an excuse or distraction, and it's time to get on with your own life."

He laughed and shook his head. "You sound like Derek. And I *have* dated, you know. I just haven't found anyone I want to go out with more than a few times. I definitely haven't met anyone I've liked enough to bring around the family. Since I don't think mail-order brides are a thing anymore, I'm not sure what you two think I should do."

Carol chuckled. "No, I hope you can find your bride somewhere other than a catalog or a website. I was thinking along different lines. Even when you were a little boy, you were always a planner and you wanted to have control. You've had your plans for your life figured out for years and God keeps showing you that He's the One in charge of planning. Maybe it's time you believed Him and trusted *Him* to prepare you and to bring her around."

"I'm not sure how to do that, Mom. I mean, of course I trust Him. I just don't know how to just *let* Him do it. I don't even know what that means."

"Well, we haven't talked about it for a long time, but what keeps coming up in my mind as I pray for you is Victoria."

He felt like cold water had just been thrown in his face. "Why would *she* come to mind? You know she's not the one for me."

"I know, honey, that's not what I mean. Seeing the look on your face when I said her name confirms what I've suspected – you're still bearing some big scars from what happened with her."

21

"You're right, but do you blame me? I dated her for eight months and it took the draft for her true colors to come out. I know that one of the things the injury saved me from was a life with someone who only pretended to love me for me, and I shudder to think what life would have been like if I had married her. The first challenge that came around might have been the end of it." He shook his head. "Actually, it was – we broke up less than forty-eight hours after the draft. Thank God the Niners called *after* she showed her true self, or the charade would have gone on for even longer."

"I know. I don't blame you for being gun-shy. She made you question everything."

"She did. She made me question women, but the worst thing was that I started questioning my instincts with people. I've forgiven her, but I still don't know how I didn't see it with her."

She looked sympathetic. "You were pretty caught up in things back then. You were so distracted by the broken records and bright lights and headlines that it's no wonder you didn't question the woman beside you."

Carol paused for a moment, leaned in, and lowered her voice. "That's not all, though, is it? We've never talked about it and we don't need to, but there were other things clouding your judgment, too. I'll be delicate here, but you weren't exactly choosing women with the purest of intentions back then."

He lowered his eyes to avoid seeing disappointment on her face. "I know."

"You know you don't have to feel ashamed with me, Clayton. Things happened as they happened and there's not a thing you can do about it now. I didn't bring it up to make you feel badly or embarrass you, but to remind you that you're not the same person you were back then, and that you have better judgment now. I'm assuming you've made things right with God about that, and it's obvious that you're nothing like you were in those days. Have you specifically asked for His forgiveness?"

"Yes, of course."

"And have you accepted it?"

Fortunately, their breakfasts arrived at the table and he got a pass on answering.

His mother put her hand on his and asked, "Would you mind if we broke tradition and I prayed for our breakfast today?"

"Sure."

"Thank you. Lord, I am so thankful for and proud of the incredible man sitting here in front of me today. I'm thankful that You brought him back to Yourself and from the direction he was going those years ago, and I ask You to heal him from all the old wounds from his own and others' sins. Please show him how to accept your forgiveness and walk with his head held high as your cleansed child. Thank You for this day and this wonderful food in front of us and please bless it to our bodies for our nourishment and health. And Lord, please teach Clayton how to trust You with his decisions in relationships, and bring his wife to him in Your way and timing. We pray these things in Jesus' Name. Amen."

"Amen. Thanks, Mom."

The image of Shelby laughing in her bridesmaid's dress with her hair piled in soft curls on the top of her head flashed before him again, and he pushed it away again. *This conversation is exactly why you shouldn't be thinking about her.*

She's way out of your league. Find someone else to think about.

His mother and brother were right. It was time to dive back into the dating pool. It was also time for some soul searching.

Chapter 5

Shelby gazed at the Marvel Point lighthouse and strained to take in every detail. It was a perfect winter day with fresh snow covering the ice along the shore and a blue sky broken up by wisps of clouds. The red roof of the lighthouse stood out in stark contrast to the snow and sky.

"Isn't it picture perfect? Do you see why this is my favorite place in Summit County?"

Jimmy, her boyfriend of five months, spoke from behind her, "It's beautiful. Now let's go find some trails." With that, he shushed past her, using his poles to try to gain speed.

"We'll see about that!" She quickly caught up to him and passed him, laughing all the way. She moved quickly over the hills until the voices of her friends disappeared behind her. After a few minutes she stopped again and gazed at Lake Michigan.

Jimmy caught up to her, slightly out of breath. "Why do you keep stopping?"

"I had to look at the lake again . . . and to let you catch up."

She giggled as she took off again. She heard him laughing behind her as he tried to keep stride with her, and his laugh again faded as she started moving ahead.

The next sight was of Clay passing her by, followed by the sound of her own breath as the race was on. The snowy scene rushed by as she gained speed and closed in on him.

She felt a tear run down her cheek and clicked *Stop* on the video.

She had a love/hate relationship with her GoPro at this point in her life. It was both wonderful and excruciating to watch the videos she used to take when she was skiing and snowshoeing and doing everything else she couldn't do anymore.When she heard Rachel come in through the front door, she quickly wiped the tears from her eyes. They had decided to start their own little book club now that Shelby had moved back to Hideaway after finally finishing college, and she didn't want her friend to see her sadness.

"Bad day? Do we need to reschedule?" *So much for fooling her.*

"No, I'm fine. I just watched the wrong video and it got to me."

"Was it one of the GoPro videos?" Rachel's voice was full of compassion, not judgment, for which Shelby was grateful.

"Yes. I know I shouldn't remind myself, but I haven't been able to get out to some of my favorite places in so long and I miss them. I just wanted to see Marvel Point – I haven't even been there since all of this started."

"You know, you can go there without skiing or snowshoeing or skating. Would you like to drive over there just to take a look, or would that be too hard?"

Shelby felt tears stinging her eyes again even as her face broke into a grin. "That would be wonderful. Do you mind?"

"I'd be thrilled to take you to your favorite place and I'm glad you're feeling well enough that you're up to it. I'll go get some travel cups so we can take our hot cocoa for the ride."

∞∞∞

It felt so good to be at Marvel Point again. She ventured out of the car and started walking slowly. Every step hurt as she worked to walk through the heavy snow, but she didn't care – it was worth it.

She walked just far enough on the path from the parking area to have a full view of the lighthouse. It was another sunny day and the lighthouse could not have looked more stately or beautiful.

"I should have brought a lawn chair so I could just sit and look at this all day. Now that I'm feeling better, I need to do this kind of stuff more often; it reminds me that I'm still alive."

"I'll bring you any time you want to come, you know. And I'm still praying that someday we'll get to come back here for snow-shoeing and skiing."

"Me too. Maybe next winter I'll be back to doing things."

"Speaking of that, what happened with the new doctor yester-day?"

"It went well. She actually listened to me, so she's better than most of the ones I've seen. She went through all of the charts and reports I brought from Tennessee, and she was surprised that I wasn't tested for more things. When I told her about how I had questioned the doctors down there and how they had basically acted like I was a hypochondriac who spent too much time on the internet, she rolled her eyes. I took that as a good sign."

"That's great! Maybe she can figure out what's going on and get you back to yourself."

"I definitely walked out of there feeling more optimistic than I've been in a while. I told her about the research I've done and about the nutritional things I've been doing, and she said that all of the things I'm doing are things she would have recommended. She gave me some more things to try, too. And yes, she even was glad that I put butter and MCT oil in my coffee, even though my friends think it's weird and gross." She giggled as she waited for Rachel to look sick.

"Oh my gosh, I forgot to tell you that my mom drinks that stuff too! She's even got my dad drinking it."

"I keep telling you, Rachel, someday you'll try it, and you'll kick yourself for waiting so long."

"We'll see about that, but it's obvious that the things you're doing are helping, because you are doing way more than you could when you first moved home. I was so glad you were able to be at my wedding and feel well enough to enjoy it."

"As much as I hated having to miss all the decorating and the rehearsal dinner, it was worth it to be able to enjoy most of your day." She smiled at her friend. "I think I need to get back in the car, but can we stay for a few minutes longer? It feels so good to be here that I don't want it to end."

"Of course. I have new pictures from the wedding to show you, too. There are some great ones of you, by the way. You looked as healthy as anyone else there."

"Well, that's a good change. I wish I could have felt as good at your mom and dad's wedding, but at least I was able to go."

Rachel pulled her tablet from the back seat and handed it to Shelby. Rachel giggled as she pointed out a picture of Clay. "Your sixteen-year-old self would have *died* if she'd seen Clayton in a tux."

My twenty-five-year-old self did *die seeing him in a tux.* She hoped Rachel didn't notice her breath catch.

Shelby tried to give equal time to each picture as they looked through them together, and fought the urge to look longer and zoom in on the pictures of Clay. *I'm just looking on behalf of my sixteen-year-old self.*

"Well, speak of the devil."

Shelby looked up and in the direction Rachel was looking in to see Clay and Mitch Huntley with snowshoes in hand, heading toward the lighthouse. Her heart skipped a beat as she watched his wide grin and confident stride, and she hoped he didn't look back and see them.

It was hard enough keeping her insides from turning into jelly when she was looking at a picture. The real thing up close and personal was more than she could take. When their eyes had met briefly while she was walking down the aisle, she had almost passed out. Their dance at the reception had just about done her in, as had the ride home from Rick and Faith's wedding, but it was totally worth it – for her sixteen-year-old self, of course.

"Do you mind if we go back now? I need to get back to my heating pad." She had never been more glad for an excuse to leave a place than at that moment.

Clay had been filling her thoughts since Rachel and Derek's wedding, and she didn't want to let on to anyone that her crush from long ago had resurrected itself the moment their eyes had met. She also knew there was no point in wasting time thinking about him. If he had never noticed her in that way when she was able to live a normal life, he certainly wouldn't now.

Chapter 6

C lay was still thinking about his conversation with his mother the week before when he arrived at his parents' house to clear off their sidewalk and driveway from the previous night's snow. His mother's car was gone, so he wasn't surprised to see his father revving up the snow blower.

"Geez, when the cat's away, the mouse will play. Step away from the snow blower, man."

Ed took on a mock dramatic tone. "Clayton Edward, I am your father. You don't get to tell me what to do. It's just a little bit of snow and I want to play with my snow blower."

"You should have thought of that before you had a heart attack and tried to die on us. You agreed to let us do this for you and it's my turn. Back away."

Ed chuckled. "Fine, have it your way. I'll go make us some coffee."

Clay hurried to clear the walk so he could have some time with his dad before his mom returned. He was always a good source of wisdom, snow blowing aside.

Ed poured the coffee while Clay took off his coat and boots. "Thanks for doing that, son. Don't tell your mother I was out there."

"Stay on my good side and your secret is safe." He laughed as they took their places at the kitchen table. He felt nervous as he spoke again. "Actually, Dad, I was wondering if we could talk about something."

"Always. What's up?"

"I'm not sure if Mom told you about our conversation last weekend, but she brought something up and it's been on my mind all week. I was hoping we could talk about it."

"Of course."

He kept his head down with his father just as he had with his mother when he talked about it, and for the same reason. "She brought up the fact that she's always known that I didn't stay on the right path with women in college, and I'm sure you've always known it, too."

"I have. I figured that when you were ready to talk to me about it, you would, and I made sure you boys knew we could talk about anything. You never did, so I left it alone and asked God to handle it with you."

Clay chuckled. "Well, He most certainly has this week. I thought I was all done with it a few years ago. I had confessed everything to Him and made a vow to Him to keep myself on the straight and narrow from that point forward, and I've kept that vow. I thought I was all done with it until Mom asked me if I had *accepted* God's forgiveness. I'm having a hard time answering that one. I've spent a lot of time talking with Him about it this week, and figured it would help to talk to you about it, too."

Ed smiled at his son. "Well, you know I've had to ask for and accept a lot of forgiveness myself in these past months, and had a harder time accepting than asking, so I guess you're in the right place. What do you think gets in the way for you?"

"I don't know, Dad. I guess I'm still stuck on the fact that I knew better. I didn't just fall into bad behavior innocently or naively. You taught us better and I thumbed my nose at it. I have no excuse."

"What do excuses have to do with forgiveness?"

"Good point. I know that God knows how much I regret it and my head knows I'm forgiven, but I just still feel unsettled lately."

"And why do you think it's coming to mind more now?"

An image of Shelby flashed in his mind again – sweet, pure Shelby.

He rubbed his face with his hands to try to get the image out of his mind. "Well, just between us, there's someone who I can't get out of my head lately. Don't get your hopes up, because she's off-limits for a number of reasons. It's just that when I think of someone like her, I think I'm just way too undeserving. I feel like I messed up any hope of having someone like that, like I would soil them."

"You know that's not how it works, son. I suppose it shouldn't be surprising that you're looking for the scoreboard, but there isn't one. The scoreboard got wiped clean when you asked for forgiveness."

"My head knows that."

"Let me ask you something. How would you feel if I didn't accept the forgiveness and the love you and your mom and your brother so graciously offered me last fall?"

"Devastated."

"Why?"

"Because I love you and wanted you to have your life and your family back. I knew you were sorry for sliding down a bad path and I didn't think twice about it."

"So, what's the difference?"

"You didn't do what I did."

"I made my wife and sons hate to be around me. Derek almost moved out of town to get away from me. That was pretty bad."

"You were doing your best. You got caught up in fear and anger, but you were trying to save your company and make things solid for us."

Ed looked at him intently. "Don't make excuses for me, Clayton. I turned into a tyrant. I don't make excuses for it, and God didn't make excuses for it. He just forgave me, just like you did. You forgiving me didn't make it okay, it made it forgiven. I have to live with the consequences of hurting the people I love the most, and you have to live with the consequences of what you did. God took away the guilt, though, and just like you wanted me to have my life and family back, God wants you to have your life and future back. So do I. And for what it's worth, when you find someone special, maybe you should let *her* decide if you're deserving of her. Don't take her choice in the matter away."

They heard Carol's car pull into the driveway and looked back at each other.

"Thanks, Dad."

"Any time, son. You know I'll be praying for you. And maybe the lady who has caught your eye isn't so unavailable."

"She is, and that's why I finally agreed to let Mrs. Andrews set me up with the woman she's been wanting me to meet. Maybe if I meet someone I like, I'll get the other one out of my head."

Ed looked as if he was about to ask more about it when the door opened. Carol was all smiles when she walked in with the groceries, and Ed took them from her hands. "Thank you, honey. I'm glad you're here, Clayton. I was sure your father would try to clear the snow today when I was gone."

Ed tried to act innocent. "Who, me? I'm just over here unloading the groceries."

"I cleared the snow and he made the coffee. Can I help with any other bags?"

"Yes, there are a few more in the trunk. Can you stay for lunch?"

"Sure. I'm having dinner at Derek's, so lunch here will make my day complete." He laughed and rubbed his stomach. "Who says single guys never get home cooking?"

∞∞∞∞

Clay looked at the screen on his phone again. His finger hovered for a moment before he hit the *Home* button. *Nope, not ready for app dating, at least not yet; anyway, I have a date in a few days.*

When Mrs. Andrews had cornered him at church, he had run out of excuses to avoid letting her set him up with one of her co-workers, and he was desperate for something to take his mind off of the one he couldn't have. He knew nothing about the woman other than the fact that she was active at her church in Traverse City and worked in the same dentist's office as Mrs. Andrews, who had assured him that he would think she was 'just darling'.

He noticed the time and realized that he needed to get out the door if he wasn't going to be late getting to Derek and Rachel's for dinner. He grabbed a bottle of Bellows Vineyards Winter White and headed out the door.

Derek looked as happy as Clay had ever seen him when he opened the door and invited him in. Clay hadn't expected a crowd, but told himself that he shouldn't have been surprised that Shelby and Brianna were there. *I suppose I need to get used to this. This is all the more reason to stop these thoughts. Lord, help me to remember that Shelby is my sister-in-law's best friend, even if it is up to her to decide if she's out of my league.*

He carefully avoided getting too close to her, just in case, and took a seat at the opposite side of the table when it was time for dinner. Rachel and Derek had made a tenderloin, or at least Rachel had and Derek had gotten out of the way, and they were excited to share a good meal with the people they were closest to. After Derek prayed for the meal and he and Rachel began serving everyone, they shared a look. *Uh-oh, is there going to be an announcement? Already?*

"Rachel and I would like to propose a toast to the three of you. You propped us up for the long, dark three and a half years that we were apart, and we just wanted to express our gratitude to you for everything you did for us – you all got us through. This meal is a small token of how much we appreciate you. Thank you." Derek gave a quick nod in Clay's direction as they all clinked glasses, and Clay breathed a sigh of relief. *Lord, forgive me for being relieved that they're not starting a family yet. Please bless them with that in Your perfect timing, even if it's next week.*

They shared stories and laughs and talked about the goings-on in town and about the treatment center for chronic pain and addiction that Rachel's parents were starting that was modeled after the one her mother had found healing in, and somehow the conversation turned to Shelby's health. She described the testing she was undergoing and Clay was shocked to learn about the number of doctors she had seen before returning home.

He was overwhelmed with compassion for her and filled with a whole new respect for her ability to remain happy and optimistic, along with bewilderment about why no one could give her answers. She seemed in need of a plan, and he was good at planning. It had turned his life around when she had given him the push a few years back. It got him back to life. He finally saw his opportunity to return the favor.

As he asked questions and tried to get an understanding of what she had done to get better and what was in the way of it happening, she seemed to wilt in front of him. He realized he had unwittingly stepped on a land mine, but instead of *him* getting hurt by that land mine, it was her. He felt like a cad and vowed to help her. He stopped asking questions and focused on listening and memorizing what she was saying. When he got home that night, he made notes of the things she had said and started Googling.

Chapter 7

Shelby had a fresh pad of paper and her favorite pen ready when Dr. Harden walked into the room. She looked serious and Shelby geared up for whatever she had to say.

She was sympathetic as she began, "Well, Shelby, the good news is you're not a hypochondriac." Shelby laughed nervously and braced herself for the bad news.

"The bad news is that you've got Lyme disease." Shelby's heart sank. That was one of the worst possibilities that they had discussed. It was also the one that she had been told time and again *wasn't* a possibility.

"Are you kidding? I told the doctors in Tennessee how much time I spent in the woods hiking and with Cross Country, and they said I absolutely didn't have Lyme disease because I didn't have the bull's-eye rash."

She fought tears as she continued, "I begged them to test me and even treat me for it just in case, and they acted like I was hysterical." *This could have been prevented.*

Dr. Harden seemed to hold her breath – or maybe her tongue – before continuing. "I'm sorry, Shelby. I apologize for my profession. As a whole, we're way behind on this stuff."

"I'm glad *you* aren't." She continued to fight against the tears, but didn't have the energy to try to stop them. Instead, she pushed through and tried to speak coherently despite them. "I don't even know what to ask you, because that's one thing I didn't spend as much of my research time on."

"That's okay. You don't have to know everything about this yet, just like you didn't have to convince me that you've been very sick."

Shelby felt relief at having someone in the medical profession listen to her and take her seriously for a change. Now that she had a real answer, she needed a goal to focus on. She pushed again to speak.

"Okay, so what do we need to do?"

"I'm glad you asked, because this is where I have good news. I've had success treating people with a protocol that starts with boosting up your system with an anti-inflammatory diet and supplements and getting your body's detox pathways in shape before going into the heavy detoxing. Sound familiar? Everything that you've been doing on your own for the last several months has been doing just that, which is why you already feel much better than you did for so long. You started the protocol before you ever walked into my office."

Shelby brightened a bit and chuckled. "So, not being able to eat bread and drinking mushroom tea and disgusting kale smoothies haven't been a waste of time?"

Dr. Harden chuckled along with her. "Far from it – you've put yourself way ahead in the game. Between that and the fact that you're young, you'll do fine. This isn't a quick fix and I can't guarantee that you'll get back to the health you had before, but I think you're going to feel significantly better than you feel now within the next several months. Now that we know what we're dealing with, we can step up the detox appropriately."

Shelby felt so exhausted when she walked out of the office that it felt like every cell in her body had a tiny little weight in it. She was relieved to have an answer and some direction for the first time, but she was so worn out by the discussion with Dr. Harden and her anger that so much of what she'd gone through – that she'd lost – could have been prevented that she needed to sit for a minute.

She still hadn't gotten used to the effect that emotional stress could have on her. A difficult conversation could make her feel like she'd just been shot up with a drug. She was glad the lobby in the large office building had seats and a waterfall she could sit by. She decided to sit with her eyes closed for a moment to try to get rid of the nausea and lightheadedness that had descended so she could be ready for her forty-minute drive home. She sat down, rested her head on her hand, and closed her eyes. *Just for a minute.*

Chapter 8

C lay couldn't wait to get back to the office to fill Derek and his dad in on the proposal the law firm upstairs had accepted. It would make them a much more attractive firm to work for, which would lure good employees, and it was a big contract for the Cooper Agency. *Win-win.*

As he stepped off the elevator, he saw someone who looked like Shelby sleeping in a very uncomfortable-looking position in a chair by the waterfall. As he looked again, he realized it *was* Shelby; she looked so vulnerable sitting there. He wasn't about to leave her there alone with people walking in and out of the lobby, so he quietly made his way over to her and sat across from her.

He answered emails while he sat with her, and he found himself looking up at her often. It felt good to sit there and watch over her for a few minutes, and he told himself that it was all in the name of friendship.

Looking at the time, he wondered how long he should let her sleep. He didn't want her to be late for an appointment, but she looked so exhausted that he figured she must need it. He decided to give her ten more minutes and tried to focus back on his emails.

When he finished the ones he absolutely had to answer, he spent a few minutes praying for her, then resumed the research he had started a few nights before after the dinner at Derek and Rachel's. There had to be something out there that could help her, and he was determined to find it.

As he was reading, a notification with the verse of the day from his Bible app caught his attention and he clicked on it.

> *Our sins are washed away and we are made clean because Christ gave His own body as a gift to God. He did this once for all time. (Hebrews 10:10)*

He looked heavenward. *Good one, Lord.*

As he was reading over the verse again, Shelby started to wake. When she opened her eyes, she looked disoriented.

"Good afternoon." He smiled at her gently.

She looked around as if trying to figure out where she was, and it looked as if every movement hurt. "Clay, what are you doing here? How long was I asleep?"

"I'm not sure how long you were asleep before I came down from my meeting, but I've been here for about twenty minutes. Are you okay?"

She looked around, dazed, and blinked several times as if trying to focus. It was scary seeing how weak and frail she looked. She looked like a different person from the smiling, joking woman he was with a few nights before.

"Please tell me your nap started *after* your appointment."

She just nodded.

"Good. I'm driving you home. Do you feel like you can walk to the parking lot?"

She nodded again. "You don't have to drive me home, Clay. I'll be fine. I just needed a moment."

He couldn't help but laugh. "Yes, that's obvious. You're totally fine."

He stood and offered her his arm. "Come on, you can sleep on the way home and I'll take care of getting your car back to you."

He tried to ignore the spark that went up his arm when she took it and used it to steady herself. He couldn't ignore how light and weak her touch felt.

He'd never seen anyone who hadn't been drinking look so out of it after a nap. As Shelby got settled into the passenger seat of his car, he slyly sent a quick text to Rachel telling her what was going on and asking if she thought Shelby needed to go to a hospital.

"No, these crashes happen sometimes. She'll be okay. I'll meet you at her house and ask Derek to drive you back to get her car if you're sure you don't mind."

"No problem. ETA 40 minutes."

It felt as if there was a giant fist clenching his chest. *This happens sometimes? This is not a big deal? Lord, what is wrong with her? Please help her. Please help me help her.*

In that moment, he felt like he would do anything to make her okay – as a friend, of course.

"Clay, can I ask a favor?"

Anything. Absolutely anything. "Of course, what do you need?"

"Would you mind stopping so I can get some Vernors?"

"You've got it." He pulled into the first gas station he saw and got one for her. While he was standing in line, he sent a quick text to Toni, the woman he was supposed to have a date with later that evening, apologizing and telling her that an emergency had come up with a good friend.

As Shelby took a sip, she coughed. "Oops. The first sip always gets me." She couldn't quite manage a giggle, but she was sounding more like herself.

"Are you feeling more awake? What happened back there?"

"I had my appointment with the doctor I told you all about, the one who's been doing all the testing. She said I have Lyme disease."

"Well, that's probably good to get a diagnosis, right? Do we need to stop to fill a prescription?"

His relief that the doctor had figured it out was stopped in its tracks by the fact that his questions seemed to bring on tears. *Another land mine?*

"The time for a prescription that could stop this thing passed years ago. The time for it to be treated and done with and for me to get back to the life I had and had planned *also* passed years ago."

He could hear the anger through her tears.

"I told them to check for Lyme. I *begged* them to treat me. They tried to give me antidepressants and sent me away. They acted like I was a hypochondriac and they ruined my life."

Clay felt powerless as she put her head in her hands and began to cry.

He could barely hear or understand her when she continued, "This could have been prevented. I could have been treated and gotten back to cross country and physical therapy and working as a trainer. This took everything away and *should* have been prevented."

"Is there anything this doctor can do for you?" *This can't be right. There has to be something.*

She took a moment and seemed to get her composure back, but it sounded like every word took effort. "She has a whole protocol that she's had success with, and she said she'll do the detox slowly so I don't go backwards, so that helps. It's just going to be a slow process. I've lost so much time already and those doctors in Tennessee wouldn't listen to me. I told them it was Lyme and they told me I was spending too much time on the internet."

She got quiet as her tears returned and Clay felt completely helpless. He had heard the anger rising in her voice and felt it rising in him, too. *This could have been prevented and these people didn't do anything?*

He reached over and put his hand on her arm. "I'm sorry, Shelby. I wish I could do something. What can I do?"

"Thanks. You're doing something – you're driving me home and listening to me. I can't tell you how much I appreciate that. Unless you happen to have a time machine in your garage, you're doing everything you can."

"This thing really took everything from you, huh?"

Her sad laugh was surprisingly empty of bitterness. "Only if you count my scholarship, my sport, my friends, my almost-fiancé, and my future. Actually, it didn't take everything. God showed me He was by my side through the whole thing, and Aunt Evelyn and Rachel and Brianna stuck by me even though they didn't understand what was going on either."

"I'm familiar with losing the sport and the almost-fiancé. You really lost friends because of this?"

"Well, when you're too tired to do anything, people sort of move on. I didn't have the energy to be around people. Pretty much everyone labeled me as depressed and wanted me to take antidepressants. The rest thought I just suddenly changed. They didn't get that I was just tired and hurt all over."

Suddenly her tone brightened. "Rachel and Brianna eventually got it. Sometimes I fell asleep during our conference calls and sometimes I just listened because I didn't have the energy to talk, but they never cut me out. Thank God for texting – that was the only form of communication that didn't immediately exhaust me."

"I'm glad they stuck around and I'm sorry things were so rough for you."

"Thanks. It's okay, I got through. What about you? How did you handle it when you lost everything?"

"I got angry and shut down. When I went from NFL prospect to just a guy, I lost the almost-fiancée, which turned out to be a gain, by the way, and I lost the joy of listening to sports radio when the talking heads turned me into a cautionary tale. But in the end, I didn't lose everything, either. My family was great, especially Derek, Mitch was great, and God brought me back from the wrong direction I was heading in."

"How did you handle it when your body let you down?" The sadness in her voice was almost too much to take.

"Well, my situation was a lot different from yours. I *caused* my injury. You didn't. I spent a lot of time beating myself up. I still do sometimes."

"Why would you beat yourself up for that?"

"Because I took the big risk that took me out of the game and the NFL."

"But that was what made you such a great player – you took risks and made the games worth watching. If you hadn't gotten hurt, the talking heads would have used you as a role model, not an object lesson. That's just the way life goes sometimes." She half-giggled and sounded almost like herself as she added, "The important thing is that you got that first down."

He laughed along with her. "You were watching?"

"Of course."

The smile they shared was one of camaraderie and friendship. The electric charge he felt when he looked in her eyes was not.

"Hopefully your losses are all behind you and this doctor will help you get your life back."

She lifted her Vernors. "Here's to that."

"Would you mind if I prayed for you?"

"I would love that."

He prayed for her strength and healing and for her doctor's wisdom and skill in treating her. He asked God to comfort her and take away the pain from all that she had lost. Getting carried away and forgetting she was listening, he thanked God for putting him in the same building so he could help her. When he realized it, it was too late and he decided he didn't care.

"Thank you, Clay. Prayer and friends are the only things that have kept me going. It means a lot to talk about this with someone who doesn't assume I lost my faith and who knows what it's like to lose their entire future because their body failed them."

"I'm sorry you had to join the club no athlete wants to join. It's the risk we take when the futures we plan depend on our bodies being healthy."

It took everything in him to stop himself from reaching over and holding her hand or pulling the car over and holding *her*. It was probably good that they were entering Hideaway.

When they pulled into her driveway, Rachel was there waiting. Shelby had gotten enough strength back that she was able to walk into the house on her own after a hug from Rachel. Rachel stayed with Clay for a moment.

"I'm so glad you were in that building. Thank you for taking care of her."

"I'm glad I could help. That has really happened before?"

"Yes. She's usually down for a few weeks after these. Did she say what happened at the doctor's?"

"Lyme disease."

Rachel grimaced. "That was the worst of the options. I've got to get in there. Thank you again, Clay."

"If there's anything else I can do – along with getting her car back here – please let me know."

"Oh, right, the car. Derek said he'll take you to pick it up after your meeting today. Why don't you come over for a late dinner tonight when you get back? She's going to be sleeping soon and will be out for the night, so she won't need me."

"You know I never turn down a home-cooked meal. See you later." He took a last look at the house and walked to his car.

He felt empty, like he'd just dropped a ball. *There has to be something that can be done.*

Chapter 9

When Shelby woke up, her first thought was of the day before. *Lyme disease – the thing that could have been treated if they would have listened to me.*

She looked at the clock and saw that she had slept for fourteen hours; she hoped that would help her recover from the day before. She didn't feel rested, but then, she hadn't felt rested after sleeping for over five years.

She thought back to the day before in the lobby of the office building and Clay's car and shuddered. *I cried like a baby in front of Clay. How embarrassing.*

She looked at her phone and saw that she missed a text message the night before from a number she didn't recognize. "Shelby, it's Clay. Your car is in your driveway and a pack of Vernors is in the kitchen in case you need it. Let me know if you need anything else. I hope you're feeling better and I'm praying for you."

I got a text message from Clay Cooper! Her sixteen-year-old self was screaming inside of her. The twenty-five-year-old who'd had a complete meltdown in front of him was mortified.

He must think I'm a basket case. Well, I can't say he hasn't noticed me now.

"Thanks again, Clay. I owe you one. I hope I didn't freak you out too much."

Just as she was second-guessing what she'd sent, her phone rang.

"Hi Brianna."

"Are you okay?"

"I'm okay. You talked to Rachel?"

"Yes, she filled me in. I'm so sorry. Want me to drive up this weekend?"

"No, but thank you. I'm going to be down for the count for a while, but you know I appreciate the thought."

"Did Clay really drive you home? How did *that* go?"

"Oh my gosh, I'm so embarrassed. I had a total breakdown in his car. I couldn't stop crying."

"I'm sure it will be okay. He's probably forgotten about it by now."

"He sent me a text last night after he dropped my car off. It was really sweet."

"Oh, really?" Shelby could hear the smile in her friend's voice.

"Stop that. You know it's not like that. You know *he's* not like that with me."

"We'll see. I saw the way he looked at you last weekend at Rachel and Derek's. Maybe he didn't mind helping you in your time of need at all."

I wish.

"Come on, you know guys don't look at me like that anymore and you know he never has. He was being a good friend and nice guy."

Lord, get me off of this topic. "How is your project coming? Are you ready for your meeting with your committee?"

"Nice try. Okay, we don't have to talk about you and your new boyfriend. Tell me what the doctor said."

She told her about the treatment protocol and talked about her anger over how something that could have been taken care of years before had ruined her life. Brianna had a few choice words for the doctors who had ignored her pleas, too.

When she hung up, she couldn't help but think about what Brianna had said about seeing Clay look at her. *She must be delusional. Put that out of your mind. The last thing you need is to start fantasizing about Clay Cooper again, or any other guy, for that matter.*

She thought about the conversation they'd had about losing the people they were dating when their worlds crashed down, and thought about Jimmy. He had been kind and supportive for the first couple of months, and had even taken her to a few doctor appointments. Pretty soon he came to the same conclusion that the doctors did and said she was depressed and needed to find her inner strength to pull herself out of the pit she'd slid into. Despite her weakened state, she found the inner strength to show him the door.

The relationship with Jimmy was just the first one she lost. Her teammates didn't understand why she didn't push through, her roommates thought she'd gotten lazy and said she wasn't pulling her weight in the apartment, and her professors thought she was asking for special favor to maintain her GPA while slacking off.

The last to go, and most painful, was her small group at church. They had prayed for her and checked in on her regularly at first, and some had even brought her meals and groceries. But as the months turned into a year and she was rarely able to make it to group meetings, they lost touch and it was clear that they thought she wasn't praying or believing enough. They irony of that was that she felt God's presence with her at that time more than she ever had before.

In the end, she was left with only four – Jesus, Aunt Evelyn, Rachel, and Brianna. And now it felt like Clay was joining that short list, too.

Chapter 10

C lay locked the office door behind him and texted Toni. "Confirming we're still on for 6:30 at North Hills Bistro."

"Looking forward to it!"

Lord, let her be perfect. Well, at least good enough to get my mind off Shelby. Nothing else had done that since he'd dropped her off the day before, and it didn't help that he had been up late researching Lyme Disease.

∞∞∞

Toni was everything Mrs. Andrews said she was – smart, pretty, engaging, and a good conversationalist. Clay asked the normal first-date questions and gave the normal first-date answers. He laughed at her jokes and listened to her stories and found they had a lot in common. On paper, she had all the qualities he was looking for. In reality, he was bored out of his mind and couldn't stop comparing her to Shelby or wishing he could be working on his research for her.

He was glad they'd made the date for a weeknight so that he could claim an early meeting and leave right after dinner. After walking her to her car, he told her how much he had enjoyed meeting her and wished her a good night. He carefully avoided saying anything that would sound like a promise to call her or see her again.

"What is wrong with me, Lord? If I would have met her a month ago, I would have had a great time and asked her for a second date in a heartbeat. She's a nice and pretty woman and I couldn't stop thinking about Shelby or get out of there fast enough. Please help me to get my head straight. Help me to help Shelby *as a friend* and stop thinking these other thoughts."

He paused and took a breath. "Okay, maybe I'll try the dating app. I've got to make something happen here."

Chapter 11

Shelby had just woken up from a three-hour nap when Rachel arrived with a care package of various teas and some books.

"Now that you're able to be awake long enough to read, I brought you a few books, including this one." She grinned as she held up the new Kristin Hamilton book. "We just got it in at the library today, so I grabbed it for us. You get first dibs if you want it. I also got a couple of others that should be easy reading, just in case you're up to it."

"Ooh, I'll take them. Today has been better. I only needed one big nap, which is a step up. I'm coming out of this one faster than last time, so at least that's good news."

"Great. Did you talk to Dr. Harden?"

"No, she said to wait a week and check back in with her, so I'm going to call her today. She wanted me out of the crash before I start with any of the new supplements and medications."

"You look a *lot* better than you did a week ago, and I'm glad this one isn't lasting as long as the last one. I'm going to get out of your way so you can rest and get out of it all the way. Derek and Clay said to make sure to tell you they're praying for you."

Shelby's stomach did a little cartwheel when Rachel said Clay's name. *No. Stop that.*

As Rachel was leaving, Faith walked in. Mother and daughter exchanged a look and sly smile that suggested it wasn't coincidence.

"Hi Shelby. I made you some more bath salts to help as you get back on your feet."

"Thank you, Faith. I just used up the last of the one you brought over the other day, so your timing is perfect."

"Oh, good. Listen, I know you're not up to doing anything just yet, but I have a couple of ideas for you to consider. First, the fundraiser for the treatment center is coming up in a few months, and we could use some administrative help with it. We've got a meeting of the fundraiser planning committee next week, too. If you would be interested in doing some work on the computer here at home, we've got things for you to do, and it would free me up to work on getting more donors and finalizing plans to open the doors."

"I would love that! I can do computer work any time. I don't even have to think about it. Whatever you have for me, I will do. I can't do much to help Aunt Evelyn around here because it takes too much energy and hurts too much, and I'm going stir crazy doing nothing."

"Oh, I was hoping you would say that! I'll bring over some files and show you what we need in the morning."

Faith paused as if she was deciding whether or not to say something else, then continued. "The other thing is for a few months down the road, so I want you to give it some thought and prayer, and I don't want you to give me an answer now. Between your degree in recreational therapy, your understanding of the alternative treatments we'll be using, and your personality, you would be a perfect activity therapist for the center. We won't be opening for at least a few months, and we don't know how quickly you'll recover, but as Rick and I have been praying about clinical staff, we both keep getting your face in our minds. We really want you to be a part of this."

Shelby was shocked and felt tears of joy coming. "Thank you, Faith. That means so much that you would want me. I can't commit officially to the activity therapy because I don't know what kind of state I'll be in then, but I really want to do it. If I can do it physically, I'm definitely in."

Faith hugged her. "Wonderful! Your job right now is to heal, and the administrative help will take a huge load off of me. You get your rest now, and we'll talk tomorrow."

Shelby was so touched by the offer and gesture that she felt the tears again. *A job.*

The idea of being able to work both excited and overwhelmed her. She had been helping her aunt as much as she could, and she was able to do quite a bit more than when she first got home a few months before, but she was still limited and it was frustrating. It was great to have something to look forward to and to feel a sense of purpose. It would also be great to have something to focus on other than replaying how cute and sweet Clay was when he took care of her, especially the way he prayed for her, the week before on a continual loop in her head.

The two visits had worn her out, and she pulled the blanket back up around her shoulders and fell asleep.

Chapter 12

C lay was on his way back to Hideaway after a morning meeting and another coffee date with someone he met through the dating app he'd finally used. The meeting had gone well and he felt confident that he was going to be able to put something together for the potential new client. The date, on the other hand, had gone about the same as all the others – nice girl, great on paper, no spark.

"Lord, can You please help me with this? I've been on four dates in the last two weeks and I don't want to ask any of them out again. I'm spending a lot of time with great women, and all I can think about is the one I can't have." He thought back to what his mother had said a few weeks before about letting God bring the right woman around.

"Okay, let's try something different. Mom was right when she said that I'm trying to plan and make things happen, and that I need to let You do this. I don't even know how, though. I've lived my whole life making plans and getting things done, and I don't know what it means to let You do the work. Please give me some kind of sign or direction here, and I'll follow."

As he passed through the gateway that welcomed people to Hideaway, he looked at the clock. If he went to the office, he would likely get pulled into conversations that would make him late to the meeting about the fundraiser, so he decided to go straight to Evelyn Glover's house, where the meeting was taking place. He wasn't sure why they were meeting there, but made a mental note to offer the conference room at the office for future meetings if it inconvenienced Evelyn or Shelby. He tried, unsuccessfully, not to hope that Shelby would be home.

Shelby answered when he knocked on the door, and he was relieved to see that she looked like she had recovered nicely from the crash two weeks before. As he hugged her hello, he tried not to notice how good she smelled and forced himself to keep it brief.

"You look great, Shelby. How are you feeling?"

"I'm coming along. Thanks again for the rescue that day. And I'm sorry for all the crying. When I get worn down and exhausted like that, I cry like a faucet."

"It seems to me that you've had plenty of reason to cry over these past years as you've been dealing with this. Are you doing the new detox step yet? Rachel said the doctor had you hold off on it for a while to get stronger."

She spoke as she led him into the dining room. "I'm actually starting tomorrow morning, because I don't know how it will affect me. I wanted to wait until after the meeting today, so I could participate."

He looked over at the packets laid out on the table. "You're going to be in the meeting today? Did you join the committee?"

Chill out, Cooper. You sound like a schoolgirl who just found out her crush is in her homeroom. He was sure she picked up on the excitement in his voice and smile on his face and recommitted to acting casual.

When she smiled right back, his stomach did a leap. "I actually joined the staff, so I'll be in a lot of meetings. I'm going to do administrative work to help out for now, and if I can continue to get stronger and get back to myself, I'll be joining the clinical staff as the activity therapist when the center opens."

He had to stop himself from hugging her again. "Wow, congratulations. You'll be perfect at that. You've got a lot of us praying for you and I guess we'll see what God has in store, huh?"

He was glad that the doorbell rang, because she walked away to get it just as he felt a nudge in his spirit reminding him to trust God with his relationships.

He wanted desperately to ask Him to make her the woman for him, but shook his head to clear away the thoughts. *She's off-limits. Stop trying to find ways around that fact.*

The meeting went well, and Faith delegated assignments like a pro, even though she had never organized a big fundraiser before. Pastor Ray had some good ideas, as did Shayna, a friend of Emily's who had come up from Detroit to help out as a favor to her. They quickly divided up the tasks that each committee member was to work on and spent the rest of the time praying as a group for the fundraiser and for the future clients of the center.

At the close of the meeting, Faith approached him. "Clayton, I'm so glad you volunteered to join the planning committee, and thanks again for recommending the other insurance agency to us. As much as I would have liked to have you handling our insurance, I wouldn't want to give the impression of a conflict of interest because of our relationship to Derek. The up side of that is that since you don't have a business relationship with the center, we can work on convincing you to join the board."

Clay was surprised and flattered. "I would gladly join the board if you'll have me. A lot of my teammates from college are on narcotics from old injuries that turned into chronic problems, and there are a few who seem to be completely addicted. I wish they had a place like this to go to. This is going to be a great addition to what this area has to offer, and a lot of people are going to get new chances at life through it. I'll do whatever I can to contribute, and I've already been calling contacts and telling them what we're doing here and how they can be a part of something great as we gear up for the fundraiser."

"Every fundraising committee should probably have salesmen on their team." She laughed and added, "but they can't have you – you're ours. Let's talk this week about the board."

She went to talk to Shayna to thank her for coming and Clay joined Rachel and Derek in helping Shelby clean up the room.

As they were carrying dishes into the kitchen, Derek asked Clay how his date earlier in the day had gone. Shelby was behind them and Clay turned to see a look on her face that he hadn't seen before.

Did she hear that? Is that disappointment I see?

His heart did a little leap as he wondered if he could possibly be seeing one of the signs he was looking for, then fell when he remembered she wasn't an option. *She's pure and she's Rachel's friend – that makes her off-limits times two.*

The verse about being made clean popped into his mind and he made a mental note to ask God later if she might just be off-limits times one. She was still off-limits because she was Rachel's friend, but maybe he could have a life with someone like her – if he could *find* someone else like her.

Chapter 13

Shelby felt her stomach drop as she pictured Clay smiling and charming some beautiful, healthy woman.

See? This is why you need to stop thinking about him. That's at least the third date you've heard about him going on recently. He's been sweet to you lately for the same reason he was when you were a high school freshman and he was a senior – he's just a nice guy.

Shelby got out of the kitchen as quickly as she could and hurried to get the rest of the papers organized and cleared away. She looked for a reason to get out of the room before he returned so she didn't have to look into the face of the person who had never seen her and never would.

Faith approached her and took the folders from her hands. "Shelby, you look whipped. You've been so helpful and did a great job with everything here. Now it's time for you to be done for the day and go upstairs to rest. This is why I asked to have it here, so that you could go directly to bed if needed."

She gave a gentle mom-look as she pointed toward the stairs. Shelby was glad that she assumed that the look on her face was from the physical illness rather than heart sickness.

She was relieved to have orders to leave the room and quickly said her goodbyes to Rick and Pastor Ray before the others came back from the kitchen. As she was walking into her room, Brianna called.

"How did the meeting go?"

"It was good, and they liked the ideas you emailed. Everyone is just wrapping up and leaving now. My boss told me to go to bed, so I'm just walking into my room."

"Who was there?"

"Oh, you know, the usual group – Faith, Rick, Rachel, Pastor Ray, and Emily – plus Derek, Clay, and a friend of Emily's from Detroit who has done event planning."

"Oh, really? *Clay* was there?" Brianna giggled.

Shelby had never wished for a dropped call more than at that moment.

"Brianna, stop. I keep telling you there's nothing there."

"And I keep not believing you."

Shelby wished she could tell her best friend what was in her heart. "Well, that's your choice. I really do need to take a nap, so can I call you tomorrow? Or maybe Rachel can tell you about the meeting."

"Maybe I'll ask *Rachel* if you and Clay were making eyes at each other across the table."

"*No!*"

Brianna started laughing uncontrollably. "*I knew it!* What's going on between you two? And since when do you keep anything from me or Rachel?"

"Nothing is going on, okay? And I don't want anything to be awkward now that he's Rachel's brother-in-law. I just made the mistake of letting my inner teenager come back out and get excited about being near him. There's nothing there, though. I'm still invisible to him and he's just nice to me because he's a nice guy and we're old friends. That's it, end of story." She could feel tears trying to burst forth as she again pictured him having the time of his life on dates.

"I'm sorry, Shelby. I won't tease you about it anymore. But I really did see him looking at you when we were at Rachel's, and you're most definitely not invisible to him. I'm not going to say anything more about it, but I had to say that. You get some rest and call or text me tomorrow to tell me how you're feeling."

∞∞∞

Two days later, Shelby was up at the crack of nowhere-near-dawn. "Okay, Lord, I guess this is just one of those days where I wake up at three a.m. and am up for the day. It's as good a time as any to spend time with You."

She spent time reading her devotional books and the topic of fear and vulnerability came up over and over. "Okay, I get it. I admit it – I'm afraid and feel vulnerable. I hate feeling vulnerable. I don't know what to do or how to organize my life right now.

"I don't know what to hope for or dream about. I know I can't dream about marriage and family because I don't really have anything to offer anymore, and I don't know if I can dream about a career beyond the fifteen or twenty hours per week that I can work for the center because I don't know if I'll ever get better.

"I guess I have to come up with a completely different life plan than I used to have. I need to make the most out of the life that I have and put the life that I wanted and thought I would have to rest. Please show me how to press the reset button and find a way to enjoy what I have and make it as good as it can be."

She decided that one way to enjoy her life was to create little moments and to treasure them as much as possible.

"Today I will start the day with a wonderful little moment. If I get in the car now, I can get out to Marvel Point for the sunrise."

She felt her excitement build as she drove to Marvel Point. She wasn't surprised to be the only one out there, since most people only thought about sunrises during the summer, not early April. Now that the big mounds of snow that had been there just a few weeks before were melting, she could park a bit closer to the lighthouse and she found a spot with a good view of it. She wished she had brought her camera, but as part of her plan to truly enjoy a little moment, she had left it at home, along with her phone and any forms of entertainment or distraction.

Sitting and looking at the lighthouse as the sky displayed a dizzying array of pinks and corals and splashed the snow with color, she was in awe and found herself smiling at the early sky and snow. She was so caught up in the wonder that she jumped when she heard a tap on the window.

Clay stood there smiling outside her passenger side door. He motioned to her to unlock the door and she took in a gulp of air as she hit the button.

Lord, help me.

He climbed into the car as he greeted her. "Good morning!"

"Good morning. Are you out for one last snowshoeing run?"

"I am. Mitch is meeting me here in a while. What about you? Are you plotting your eventual return to domination of Marvel Point?" He smiled in her direction and she felt lightheaded. This time it wasn't because of a crash.

She tried to maintain her composure and laughed. "I'm feeling better, but I don't think I'll be snowshoeing quite yet – maybe next year."

She looked out over the snow, longing to be able to be out there doing *something*.

"You really miss it, huh?" He suddenly sounded very serious and the way he looked at her took her off guard.

"More than words can say."

"I get it. I remember when I was rehabbing the last injury and couldn't do anything but what the trainers told me to do. It was awful. I can't imagine having to be even more limited or deal with it as long as you have."

"Awful is right. Being active – being an athlete – was such a part of who I was, and now it's tiring to drive out to my favorite place to watch other people do what I love."

A tear escaped from her eye and she quickly wiped it away before he could see it. She reminded God how much she hated feeling vulnerable and asked Him to take the feeling away.

"You're apparently a better person than I am. I couldn't stand to watch other people do what I couldn't."

He paused as he surveyed the scene outside of the car. "Life can change in the blink of an eye, can't it? Every time I'm doing something active, I remind myself I may never have the chance to do it again. Every run could be the one to take out my knee for good, so I take the risk and hope it's not the last time. Reminding myself that it could be forces me to enjoy it as much as possible"

"Hmm, that's wise."

He laughed, "Of course it's wise. *You're* the one who reminded me of that the last time we were here together."

"I did?"

"Yes, you did. You gave me the butt-kicking I needed to get back to life."

"Really?" She had a hard time believing that he remembered any conversation with her that happened years before.

He turned toward her and his face turned serious again. "Really.

You called me on playing it safe and reminded me of who I was and who I was becoming. Everyone else felt sorry for me, but you told me to stop being cautious and get back to taking risks. I stopped playing it safe, in sports at least, and the rest of my life got back to normal."

He paused and she didn't know what to say, so she remained silent. "You know, I've never told you how grateful I was for that conversation, and when you talked about all you had been going through that night at Derek and Rachel's, I wanted to return the favor to you. I wanted to give you the helpful butt-kicking you gave me."

She felt more tears stinging her eyes. *All I've gotten for five years is a continual butt-kicking from life. I can't take more from you. Please, Lord, don't let this turn into yet another conversation where someone tells me I'm not trying or believing hard enough.*

"Shelby, I owe you an apology. Up until and even after that night, I thought you weren't fighting or trying to push through. I thought you just needed a push or a plan, and I was going to be the guy to do it. That was how I was going to return the favor."

Now I get it. I was your service project. Lord, please get me out of this conversation. Doesn't he have another date to get to or something?

"When I saw you in that office building lobby and took you home, I saw how hard you were fighting. I saw that you had far more strength than I could have realized. My injury changed my life, but your illness *took* yours. I still don't understand how what happened to you that day was a regular occurrence and no one did anything to stop it. I don't get how they gave up on you and thought you weren't trying or that it was all in your head."

Shelby was shocked – and touched – that he seemed to get it, at least a little bit. She stared out the window as she tried to control the tears, knowing that if she tried to speak, they would unleash in a gush she may not be able to stop.

Chapter 14

Shelby wouldn't look at him. He had no idea what to do. He gave it a minute, hoping she would respond to his apology.

"Shelby, I'm sorry. Will you forgive me for not getting it?"

"Of course. I'm not mad, Clay. I'm used to people not getting it. It's not that big a deal anymore." She still wouldn't look at him, and he hated hearing the tears in her voice.

"What can I do to make it up to you?"

She gave a pained laugh. "There's nothing to make up for and nothing you can do, but I do appreciate the sentiment. I really do. You can keep praying for me, because that's the thing that keeps me going."

She turned her face toward him and it was obvious she was forcing her smile. She had tears in her eyes and he felt like he'd been sucker-punched.

"You should get out there and have your fun, Clay. Go do it for those of us who can't."

She sounded like a woman who had lost everything and who was desperately hanging on to avoid breaking down. It broke his heart as he pictured the bubbly, unstoppable girl she'd been before this all happened. He knew she was still in there, but she was hurting and tired and beaten down. He wanted to give her some hope, anything to hang onto.

"I will, and I see that Mitch just pulled up, but can I come over to see you later? When I saw that it wasn't a push that you needed, I started doing a little research and I found a bunch of websites and podcasts that talk about things that help with Lyme and chronic illness. I'll show you what I've found and you can decide what you want to do with it."

"Sure. I'll be around."

∞∞∞∞

That afternoon, Clay was having a hard time focusing on the work on his desk and was relieved when Rachel appeared in his office doorway.

"Hi, Clay. Derek and I are going to the Bay Shore Diner for lunch. Would you like to join us? Unless, of course, you have another lunch date." She smirked. She seemed to be enjoying teasing him about his recent dating binge almost as much as Derek did.

Clay laughed. "I'm broke after all the dates I've been on recently, and they've all been a waste of time. I would love to have lunch with you two. I won't have to work as hard, and I know I'll have a good time."

"Of all the women you've met, none of them have captured your interest?"

Not enough to take my mind off of the one that I can't have.

"Not one. I'll keep trying and maybe the next one won't bore me." He looked sheepishly at her. "I sound like a picky jerk, don't I?"

Rachel laughed, but then turned serious. "We all know you're no jerk, and you need to be picky. That's the person who is going to be by your side through everything that's going to come your way. I went out with a few nice guys who bored me to tears when Derek and I were broken up. It's kind of what I was looking for, though. I didn't want to have my heart broken again, so I chose guys who weren't that exciting. When I finally did what God said, everything changed."

"I know that I need to let God make it happen, but I don't know exactly *how* to do that. What did you do?"

"I followed the nudge to talk to Derek. I thought I needed to talk to him and get answers from him so I could move on from him. I figured if I had answers and understood, I could, and that would be that." She smiled. "The answers I got were nothing like what I expected, as you know, and that conversation led to us getting back together." There was that look of adoration again.

"I know God is asking me to trust Him, but I don't know what my action step is." *Maybe if I could get a certain person out of my mind, I could see my action step.*

She looked thoughtful. "I don't mean to speak for God, and I don't know how you might go about this, but maybe you're supposed to stop trying so hard. You always have rules in your head, and maybe you're trying to follow a rule that isn't supposed to be followed. Make sure the rules you follow are rules from God, not yourself. Maybe stop trying to force something with women you're not really interested in and ask God what your next step is."

"You're right. Thanks for the sisterly advice." He grabbed his coat. "Let's go find Derek. I'm starving."

He sat silently and prayed as he rode over to the diner with Derek and Rachel. *Lord, please show me what my action step is and please show me which rules are Yours and which are mine.*

When he realized that the rules about Shelby being off-limits were ones that he'd made in an effort to atone for sins he'd been forgiven for and to do something for Rachel that Rachel had never asked for, he felt like the sun broke through the clouds.

He couldn't wait for the afternoon to pass so that he could go to Shelby's. Maybe they could talk about more than his research.

As Derek pulled into the diner parking lot, Clay opened his phone and grinned as he deleted the dating app. *Now that's an action step.*

Chapter 15

Shelby sipped ginger tea as she tried to fully wake up. She wanted to be alert when Clay arrived and was hoping she could get through the discussion without crying. Her nervousness about what he was going to say was overwhelming her and putting her on the edge of tears.

It was always hard when people thought they had answers for her. They never seemed to think that she was doing quite enough and they always thought they had the magic bullet. It was exhausting listening to people tell her about the perfect supplement or essential oil or psalm that had cured someone they knew or read about and muster up an enthusiastic response.

It wasn't that she was against any of those things – she was for and used all of them – it was dealing with the judgment and disappointment and assumption that she just wasn't listening or trying if she didn't get as excited as they were that wore her out. She knew he meant well, but she knew that this conversation was likely to go the way many had before. *Oh well, at least if I'm dreading his visit, I'm not having childish fantasies about him coming here to declare his love for me.*

When she opened the door and saw the ten-thousand-watt grin on his face, her breath caught and she looked away when she couldn't stop her own. She reminded herself that he was being a friend and that she was just his latest project, and focused on showing gratitude that he wanted to help. She was quite sure she would melt if he gave her a hello hug, so she backed up as she opened the door and gestured toward the parlor.

"How was snowshoeing this morning?"

"It was as good as it can be in April. You know how that is."

"I don't miss trying to do winter sports in slush, but I still don't blame you for getting out there for every last possible time."

"Maybe next year you'll be out there in the slush, too." *There's that grin again. Try not to swoon.*

Returning his smile took no effort at all. "Let's hope."

He showed her his computer case and winked. "Thanks for letting me come over. I got excited when I started digging into this stuff, and wanted to share it with you in case it would help." His enthusiasm was infectious and she found herself drawn in by it.

"I appreciate you putting in the effort. What have you found?" *Lord, help me to not be sensitive to judgment and to express gratitude for what he's trying to do. And help me to focus on the topic at hand and not get too close to him.*

Just as he started to talk, the Shoreside Inn guests walked in the door. The downside of living in a home that was a bed and breakfast was that it was difficult to get much privacy when guests were there. Evelyn worked hard to make guests feel welcome and everyone loved spending time in the elegant parlor, so Shelby usually vacated it when guests were around.

She was about to ask Clay to move into the small library to continue their discussion when he looked like he got an idea.

"How would you like to end the day the way we started it? If we head over to Marvel Point now, we'll have plenty of time to go over this before the sun sets."

As they drove over, she was glad that he was filling her in on the research he'd done so she had something to focus on other than being in such close quarters with him again. *If only my sixteen-year-old self could see us riding out to Marvel Point together.*

Settle down, self. It's not like we're going on a date. That's what he does with other women. It's just a practical place to go to talk privately.

He sounded excited as he shared what he had found out about chronic illness in general and Lyme disease in particular, and he talked about inflammation and detox like he'd been in that world for years. She didn't want to interrupt as he explained things she already knew and was relieved that he hadn't found something that was billed as a quick or easy fix that she would have to gently and diplomatically reject.

"Wow, you're a quick study. I've been learning about this stuff for the past several months and you picked it up in two weeks."

He laughed and looked at her sheepishly. "I tend to get a little obsessed when I'm learning for a good cause."

He suddenly looked disappointed when he looked at her. "Wait, none of this is new information to you, is it? I was hoping I had found something helpful."

She laughed. "No, it's not new to me, but it *is* helpful. It's good information, and it's good to hear a fresh take on it from someone who is new to all of this."

"So have you been doing all of this – the diets and supplements – for months? And they're not working?"

"Actually, they *are* working. Believe it or not, I'm much better than I was a year ago. The way you saw me after my doctor's appointment is how I was almost constantly a year ago. Now it takes a lot more to get me to that point. And the fact that I'm able to be out here two weeks after a crash is huge progress."

"You've got to be kidding."

"I wish I was. The reason it took so long to get my degree is that I had to drastically reduce my course load. Even then, all I could do was go to class and sleep. I also had to change my major because I couldn't physically do it. I started out in an intensive program that would get me a Bachelor's and Master's in physical therapy in five years, and planned to use it either to do PT or to be a trainer. When the illness wouldn't go away, my advisor finally told me that I had to change to something else. Fortunately, most of my credits could count toward a recreational therapy degree, so that's what I ended up getting."

"That must have stunk to have to give up your plans like that."

"It was devastating to lose my last tie to the world of sports, but I found that I actually liked the work of recreational therapy better. I could have more fun with it and use it in different settings. I'm really hoping to keep improving so I can be the activity therapist at the center when it opens. Faith said the job is mine if I want it and can handle it." She couldn't help but smile when she thought about how good it felt to be wanted at the center.

"I'm praying for your healing, too. If God can create beautiful great lakes and sunsets like that, He can heal you enough to put you in that job."

"Yes, He can, and we'll see what His plans are for that."

Chapter 16

Clay saw his opening. He had never been nervous asking women out, but he had never asked one out who didn't give off strong hints that she would say yes.

Shelby was a different woman indeed. He saw plenty of signs that the attraction was mutual, but she was by no means falling at his feet. It was quite the opposite – if anything, she was giving him the stiff-arm.

He hoped he was reading things right and decided that he was going to take the risk. "So now that you can think about a job, do you also think about getting back to other parts of life? Friends, dating…"

She laughed. "Friends? Yes. Dating? I don't think so."

"Why not?"

She laughed again, but he saw a flash of something in her eyes that suggested a deep sadness.

"That part of my life is on permanent hold. The last thing I need is someone else who thinks I'm depressed and 'not accessing my inner strength', and I'm not really what men are looking for these days."

"You're everything some men are looking for, Shelby." *Did I really just say that? So much for subtlety.*

She looked surprised and he thought he saw her blush as she

looked back at the sun setting over the water. "That's very sweet of you to say, but I don't think so." She turned and smiled at him. "Thank you for saying it, though. You're a good friend."

He laughed and turned to face her head-on. "Are you kidding? I think we're finally going to have the butt-kicking conversation. You told me a long time ago that by being cautious with my knee, I was risking being bored to death. You were right.

"You reminded me that I was a risk-taker and it turned me around, with sports at least. The reason you could call me out on that was that you were the same way, and now you're doing the same thing I was – you're being cautious and risking being alone. Even after our conversation that day, I kept being cautious with other things, but now I'm ready to take your risk-taking advice in life. Are you?"

She giggled and sounded like the old Shelby. "What, are we playing Truth or Dare now? You're going to dare me to do something risky?"

He laughed along with her, but held her gaze. "Yes, I am. I dare you to take dating off hold and let me take you out."

A look of shock flashed on her face and he was certain he saw a touch of fear. "A *date*? You don't have to do that, Clay."

"Don't have to do what? Do you think I'm asking you on a pity date?"

He couldn't help but laugh more at the thought that *she* would be anyone's pity date. "Okay, say truth or dare."

She laughed nervously. "Okay, you've made your point."

"Truth or dare, you say? Truth."

He stared at her for a long moment. "Ask me if I really want to take you on a date."

She looked at him as if he'd lost his mind. "Clay, are you having some kind of stroke or something?"

He decided to put his money where his risk-taking mouth was and put his cards on the table to show her just how serious he was. "Yes, I do really want to take you out. I've been able to think of pretty much nothing else since Derek and Rachel's wedding."

He took her hand and looked her in the eye. "Will you go out with me? Say yes."

He smiled and waited for her answer. *Please say yes. Please say yes.*

Her shy smile sent fireworks off inside him.

"Yes."

"Tomorrow night? Dinner?"

"Yes."

Yes!

Chapter 17

I *can't believe I'm going on a date with Clay. I don't know what to wear and have no idea how this happened, but I'm going on a date with Clay.*

She hadn't said a word to Rachel or Brianna about either the conversation the night before or the date. It was weird not to tell them everything, but since it was Clay and not some random guy, it seemed best not to – not yet, anyway. She didn't want there to be any awkwardness if things didn't go well.

She was still wondering if she was dreaming or if he was just trying to make her feel good. Even if it was a real date, she couldn't figure out what had changed so drastically that he would go from not seeing her to asking her out. She hoped that if it was real, it wasn't just because he'd gone through all the women in Summit County. She sipped her ginger tea to try to settle the butterflies in her stomach. It didn't work.

Emily knocked on her door. "Your date is here. He's downstairs talking to Joe."

"Oh no! I'm not ready and I don't know what to wear."

"You look as nervous as I did when I had my first date with Joe. Take a deep breath and look in the mirror. You look great. Now, what are your options?"

"Those two dresses." She pointed to the dresses on the bed.

"Which one do you feel best in?"

"That's my favorite, but I feel funny getting dressed up."

Emily laughed. "I understand. I didn't curl my hair for our first date because I didn't want to look like I was trying too hard. He didn't even notice and gave me the best first kiss I'd ever had. Clay looks so excited to pick you up that you could wear a paper bag or a prom dress and he'll think you look perfect."

Shelby felt the heat rise in her cheeks as she imagined getting a first kiss from Clay.

"He really looks excited?"

"*Yes*, silly!"

She thought about what he had said about taking risks and grabbed her favorite dress.

Emily grinned. "Atta girl! I'll tell him you're on your way down."

Clay's smile indicated his agreement with her choice when she walked down the stairs, and he did look like he was there to pick her up for a real date. She shivered when his hand touched her shoulder as he held her coat for her to put on. Emily gave her a subtle nod and smile as they turned to walk out the door.

It had been a long time since she had been on a first date and she wasn't sure what to talk about as he started driving toward the gateway that led out of Hideaway.

He turned to her and chuckled. "So, are you from around here?"

She laughed along with him. "We don't have a lot of first date questions to ask each other, do we?"

"Thank God! I've been on way too many first dates lately, and while I was asking and answering all of the first date questions, I was wishing that I was doing this with you."

"You were?" She gave him a shy smile. "I thought you didn't notice me that way."

"Oh, I noticed you all right. Despite my best efforts, I failed at not noticing you. I told myself that I couldn't date Rachel's best friend and I wasted a bunch of time with other women who didn't take my mind off of you. I'm glad we're finally doing this."

Yes, finally! She tried to maintain her dignity while her sixteen-year-old self was screaming at the top of her lungs and dancing inside her head.

"Where are we going, by the way?"

"The Birchwood Inn. I hope that's okay – I didn't want to wear you out by driving over to Traverse City."

"It's perfect. I haven't been there since all of this started. I hope we can get a table by the fireplace."

"I called and begged them to reserve one for us this afternoon."

When he smiled at her, she felt as if she was already in front of a fire.

As soon as they were seated, he picked up his water glass for a toast. "To taking risks."

"To taking risks." *And to the best first date ever.*

Chapter 18

She looked so angelic with the fire casting a glow on her face and hair. For the first time in a long time, he was thoroughly enjoying a first date and hoping for more. With no need for small talk, conversation flowed naturally with her and it seemed like they could talk about anything.

As they talked about their athletic glory days, the irony suddenly hit him about some of his recent dating choices. He had avoided dating women who were into sports because he wanted a woman to be interested in him for himself, but it was weird to not be able to talk about something that had been such a big part of his life. It was completely different with her; she was an athlete and a fan *and* a friend who had known him long enough that she truly saw him as a person.

"This is the first time I've talked about sports on a date since I got hurt. At first I didn't want to talk about it or be seen just as a meathead jock, and then it was exhausting trying to explain to someone how important it all was to me and what a loss it was when it was all gone. I'm glad you get it, even though I wish you hadn't had to go through what you did."

"Most people don't get it being such a part of who you are. A lot of people thought for me it was the social part. It wasn't, though. It was having every area of life affected by being an athlete and being a part of a team and having a scoreboard. I had Rachel and Brianna for the social part."

"That was Mitch for me. He got back from Afghanistan right before I got cut by the Niners, and neither of us wanted to be around crowds, so we hung out a lot at his house. He couldn't be around all the noise and sudden activity and neither of us wanted to have to answer questions or make small talk. It worked out great for both of us and we both got through the toughest time of our lives. For me the assumption people had was that I was only down because I'd lost my NFL career. They didn't get how angry I was that my body let me down or how much I beat myself up for causing it."

He knew it was his duty to give her a hint about what was in his past, and seeing that he had his opportunity, he willed himself to push the words out and get it over with before the stakes got higher.

"I never told anyone but Derek and Mitch, but I was also struggling with anger and shame for wandering from God and my morals – that was harder." He watched her face and held his breath as he waited for her reaction.

She had such compassion when she looked at him. "Ouch, that sounds much more difficult than losing physical ability. Good thing God is always there to take us back when we mess up."

When she reached over and squeezed his hand, he felt like both his earthly and heavenly fathers were saying 'we told you so.'

So she's really not off-limits.

When the waiter brought their dinners, Clay took the opportunity to lighten the conversation. "And now you're about to start a new career. Are you excited?"

"Well, I'm not one hundred percent sure if I'll be able to do it, but I've been doing some planning, just in case." She looked at him and giggled. "Okay, I've pretty much got half of my programming worked out."

"That's what I figured. You've never done anything halfway."

"You know the old saying – if it's worth doing, it's worth doing well."

He raised his glass for another toast. "To the future part-time, then full-time activity therapist. The clients are going to love you."

She met his glass with hers. "And to the overachieving new board member who has gotten more donations for the fundraiser than anyone else so far."

"Is that a competition, too?"

She grinned at him. "Isn't everything?"

He laughed. "Yes, it is. And I'm winning tonight."

"Me too."

∞∞∞∞

He didn't want the night to end, but he could see that she was getting tired.

"I should get you home. I don't want to wear you out too much."

"I'm sorry. I'm having a great time and don't want to go home, but I'm about to drop."

"I can see that. I promise I won't even feel offended if you fall asleep on the drive home. Next time we'll eat earlier."

He grinned and winked at her. "See what I did there? 'Next time'... I assumed the close."

She laughed and turned her head to the side as she met his gaze. "Next time I'll be more rested up."

She doesn't even have to have energy to be enchanting. Thank You for this night, Lord.

She stayed awake for the ride home, but it was obvious she was pushing herself to keep talking. The twenty-minute ride went quickly, and they were in front of her house before he knew it – or wanted to be.

"I'm starting to regret taking you someplace so close to home. I would have liked a longer ride."

"Me too."

As they walked toward her house, he asked, "Did you tell Rachel we were going out tonight?"

"No, I didn't want to make it weird in case it didn't go well."

He chuckled and stopped her on the sidewalk so he could look into her eyes. "And what about now? Did it go well?"

She laughed. "I'll be telling Rachel and Brianna tomorrow how much I'm looking forward to our second date."

"That's what I want to hear." He grinned as he took her hand in his and walked slowly up the porch steps.

When they got to the front door, she turned to him and smiled. "It's weird that it's not weird, right?"

"It kind of is. I had a great time tonight. I'll call you tomorrow to see when you'll be up to our second date, and I'll be praying it's soon."

He hugged her good night, and for the first time found it hard to hold to his promises to God about kissing women. *Give me strength, Lord.* He kissed her hand and gave a slight bow as he left her in the doorway and walked away while he still could.

The date had gone even better than he had thought it would. He hadn't imagined that it could have the thrill of a first date *plus* the ease and comfort of a hundredth.

He almost skipped as he walked to the car. *Now that's what a first date is supposed to feel like. Lord, please give her good rest so that we don't have to wait long for the second . . . or the hundredth.*

Chapter 19

Shelby was so exhausted when she got home that she walked straight to her room and fell asleep with a big smile on her face. She was glad for the weekly Saturday morning conference call she had with Rachel and Brianna in the morning and couldn't wait to tell them about her date.

The three best friends had started conference calls when they were all at different colleges, and even though they had them on different days and times through the week, they always had them on Saturday mornings. They all had their coffee and made an event out of it. Pretty soon Brianna would be done with her MBA program at Michigan, and Shelby hoped she would return to Hideaway and they could have Saturday coffee together in person.

When they started the call, Brianna and Rachel had lots of questions about how she was feeling, and Brianna had lots of questions for Shelby and Rachel about how the fundraiser planning was going. When they all finally took a breath, Shelby shared her news.

"So, I have something to tell you about what I did last night."

"Slept twelve hours? Stop bragging." With Brianna being in the final weeks of school, sleep was securely on the back burner for her.

Shelby giggled and took a breath. "Actually I only needed ten, so I'm improving. But before I had all those hours of sleep . . . I went on a date with Clay."

"*What!?*" Rachel and Brianna exclaimed in unison.

"You and Clay finally had a date?" The grin was obvious in Brianna's voice.

"Wait, what? *Finally*? How did I not know about this?" Rachel sounded perplexed.

"He asked me out Thursday night and I didn't say anything yesterday in case it was weird."

Rachel laughed. "Wow. We were just talking on Thursday afternoon about how he wasn't interested in the women he'd been meeting lately. I could tell he was holding back and thought he might be thinking about someone. It was *you!*"

"Did he ask you out for a second date, or was this a one-time thing?" Brianna was always good at getting right to the point.

"Yes, he asked me out for a second date, and he was so sweet."

"I *told* you he liked you."

Rachel sounded more confused. "How did you know? How did I miss all of this?"

"You missed it because you're newly married and only notice your husband, *as it should be.* I saw the way Clay looked at her at your house when you made dinner for us, but she didn't believe me. Oh my gosh, you two could be sisters-in-law!"

Shelby giggled as she tried to rein them in. "Whoa, slow down. We just had one date. He had to bring me home at eight o'clock so I could pass out, so he might still decide this is not the relationship for him. Still, it was fun to be with him and he was really sweet."

"Yeah, you mentioned that." Brianna giggled, but then turned serious. "Shelby, you may not know it, but he seems to think you're special. Enjoy it and see where it goes."

"If the look I saw in his eye on Thursday is any indication, Brianna is right. He's a good man and he's looking for a wife, not a plaything. He's ready for quality – that's you. And I'm not jumping to conclusions, but I would like nothing more than to have you as my sister-in-law."

"Okay, obviously Rachel isn't going to ask, so did he try to kiss you?"

Shelby touched her hand where he had kissed it and blushed again as she imagined him kissing her lips. "He was very gentlemanly and kissed my hand when he left. It was very—"

"*Sweet!*" Rachel and Brianna were again in unison as they finished her sentence, then all three dissolved into giggles. It was good to finally share about him, and it was especially good to have something to talk about that didn't involve a certain illness.

The conversation tired her, as always, and as she drifted off into her first nap of the day, she replayed every moment of the night before ... again.

∞∞∞∞

When she went downstairs for lunch, she was surprised to see a bouquet that included plenty of fresh lavender in the parlor with her name on it. She grinned as she opened the card.

"Thank you for giving me a first date that's worthy of flowers. Hopefully these will help you to rest up so we don't have to wait too long for Date #2." *Hopefully.*

Just then her phone rang. It still seemed unreal to see his name pop up on the screen and she couldn't stop the grin on her face.

"Hi, Clay. I'm just looking at some really beautiful flowers. Thank you."

"Well, they were inspired by you. Has that lavender worked yet? Are you rested up and ready for our second date?" She swooned as she pictured the smile on his face when he laughed into the phone.

She laughed along with him. "I wish it worked that fast, but I think I'll be on the couch in front of movies today."

"Would it be too much if I brought dinner to you and we watched a movie together?"

It would be my dream Saturday night. "That would be great."

"Okay, how about if I come over at five-thirty? But you have to promise me you'll kick me out when you get tired."

"I promise."

Chapter 20

C lay almost skipped again as he walked up the porch steps for the second night in a row. He could definitely get used to having his dinners with Shelby.

She looked tired but beautiful as she answered the door and invited him in. He gave her a quick hug and showed her the bags of food he'd brought from the Fresh Green Café. The chef was an old friend and she'd whipped up a special meal that fit all of the dietary guidelines Shelby was following.

Everything flowed easily again and Clay enjoyed having another conversation that didn't require effort to show interest in. They had known each other for so long and had such history with each other, even being different ages, that one topic flowed into the next.

"That dinner was delicious. Thank you again, and please give my compliments to Miranda."

"I will. How about if you go sit on the couch and pick a movie for us while I take care of the leftovers? Nothing too sappy, please."

She chuckled. "I don't like sappy, either, so that will be easy. I'll find something we'll both like."

"I'm really just here for the company, so I'll be happy with whatever you pick." He winked as he gathered the remnants of their dinner and headed into the kitchen.

When he walked into the parlor five minutes later, Shelby had the movie cued up and was sitting on the couch. "That didn't take long."

"Quick clean-up is one of the benefits of takeout. Did you find something for us?"

"Yup, I found something light and sap-free." She had a twinkle in her eye that intrigued him.

"What is it?"

She smirked and clicked *Play.* She giggled as he saw Lake Michigan come into view, then the Marvel Point lighthouse, and realized it must be a GoPro video she took. Clay laughed when her old boyfriend Jimmy appeared on the screen.

"Are you trying to make me jealous? Because while I'm envious of every minute that guy got to spend with you, I'm the one here now, so I win."

She just laughed and said, "Keep watching."

The way was clear in front of the camera and it was obvious she was enjoying the snowy scene and the lake – and that she was ahead of the crowd. Suddenly he could hear someone approaching and saw himself pass her.

"Yes! Go, me!" He raised his arms in victory.

She kept laughing as he watched himself create distance, then watched her catch up to him.

"Go, *me!*" She raised her own arm.

"You were always the only one in that group who had a chance to catch me." He turned toward her and reached out his hand as he gave her a cheesy grin. "But now I'm trying to catch you."

"Awww." She giggled as she took his hand. "I think you already have."

"Do you remember that day? That was the day you told me to stop being cautious. That was a great day."

"This is a great day, too, because this time when I'm watching, it makes me smile instead of feeling sad that I can't do this stuff right now. I don't know if I'll be racing, but I'll be back out there next year."

"I believe you will. Want to watch it again?"

As she attempted to say yes, a yawn interrupted her.

"Uh-oh, that's my cue to leave. I wouldn't want to get in the way of you resting up for our third date." He laughed as he said, "Oh, look! I did it again."

"Yes, you did. I'm sure my lavender will help me rest up for our third date."

Chapter 21

Shelby was almost as nervous getting ready for her morning date as she had been the first night they'd gone out two weeks before.

He didn't tell her what they were doing, but told her to dress for outdoor activity and to bring her GoPro. They had seen each other every day and she was having the time of her life.

She tried to ignore how strangely her clothes fit her. Even though she was building muscle tone back, she didn't feel like she was in *her* body. She reminded herself to give it time.

He had joined her on a few of her daily short walks and she was building her strength back up, but she was nervous about what he had in mind for the day. She wanted so badly to be able to do whatever it was he was planning and once again wished she was back to her old self. She took a breath and thanked God for giving her the strength that she had.

When she opened the door, he was down on the sidewalk doing his best spokesmodel pose in front of a tandem bike. "What do you think? I borrowed it from my neighbor and she promised me that the person on the back didn't have to do any hard work. Are you up for it?"

A sigh of relief escaped with her laughter at the sight. *I can do this.*

"Did you purposely get a tandem bike so that I can't pass you?"

His laugh made her heart leap. "I'm not gonna lie – that is an added benefit. It's lady's choice today. Would you like to ride around town, or put this in the back of my car and head over to a trail?"

"Ooh, trail, please!"

"The lady has made an excellent choice. When given the choice between two places to ride, always choose the one with more trees."

Shelby was thrilled to get out in nature again, and touched that he had figured out a way to get her there. They went to the trail that used to be a railroad track and led from Hideaway to Sapphire Lake and then into Lakes End. Once they got on the trail and were surrounded by trees and nature, Shelby felt like she was living her own life again, rather than some strange parallel version. She took in the fresh air and stream and small animals and soaked in every sight and smell.

"You never cease to amaze me, Clay. Thank you for bringing me here."

"You'll come here on your own bike or legs someday, but in the meantime, Mrs. Watson said I can borrow this any time."

∞∞∞

Recovery from the tandem bike adventure took less time than she feared it might. Clay's birthday celebration with his family the next weekend was the first time she would be joining in on a Cooper family game night, and she wanted to be ready for it. She spent the week getting as much rest as she could in between seeing him and working on the fundraiser for the center, which was only seven weeks away.

The evening with Clay's family was full of laughter, stories and good-natured competition, and she loved being part of the closeness his family shared. Rachel had always felt welcomed as part of the family when she and Derek were dating, and Shelby could see why. They were a special group. It reminded her of the old days before her parents died and filled her with fond memories.

As Clay blew out the candle on his cake, his mother leaned over and whispered, "I think Clayton already has his wish."

Chapter 22

C lay was having the best birthday ever. The celebration with the family the night before had been fun, made much better by having Shelby there at his side.

She fit in great with his family, and was even able to keep up with his father's quick wit and teasing. Ed had expressed his hearty approval when Clay confirmed his suspicion that Shelby was the woman he had told him about, and had assured him of his continued prayers.

She fit in perfectly when the games began, just as he knew she would. She also proved to be his perfect teammate, as he also knew she would.

After they won a few rounds of Sequence, Derek started complaining. "It doesn't seem fair that the two most competitive people in Summit County are on the same team."

Rachel chimed in, too. "Summit County? Try the state of Michigan."

Clay looked at Shelby and laughed. "Team Newlywed are a couple of whiners."

"No kidding!"

Ed and Carol looked around the table as they laughed so hard they couldn't speak. Finally Ed spoke up. "As the man of this house and patriarch of this family, I'm making an executive decision and breaking up the Dream Team. I don't care if it *is* your birthday, Clayton. The next game is boys against girls."

Everyone whooped and hollered and started in on the trash talk except Shelby. She just smiled at Clay with the terrifying smile of someone who was determined to win at all costs.

Ed turned to Shelby. "As the family game night rookie and the woman who is about to experience her first loss of the evening, you choose the game."

Derek piped up. "And no fair choosing Charades. You and Rachel know how to read each other's minds."

Shelby looked innocently at Ed and batted her eyes.

"Charades, please."

Best family game night ever.

He was glad it had worked out to have the family celebration the night before so that he could spend his actual birthday alone with Shelby eating dinner and watching a movie. The next week was another hard-core rest week for her so that she could be fully ready for Joe and Emily's wedding the following weekend, and he wanted to have as much time as he could with her before the official rest time started.

He had requested a simple meal of steaks on the grill and some vegetables, and he was once again impressed by her ability to make a delicious meal out of foods that were safe for her. As he manned the grill, he watched her work through the kitchen window and felt a warmth flow through his chest. *I could definitely get used to this . . . I already have.*

After dinner he insisted on doing the dishes while she found a movie for them to watch. When he walked into the parlor, she had cued the movie up, but had fallen asleep on the couch. He shifted her and put a pillow under her head so she would be more comfortable, and carefully sat on the other end of the couch, pulling her feet onto his lap and covering her with a blanket.

He sat and watched her and prayed for everything that came to mind for her health and happiness. She stirred briefly when her Aunt Evelyn came through the door after having dinner with the Callahans, but didn't fully wake.

Evelyn looked at her as she sat down on the settee across from the sofa. "It looks like you lost your date in the middle of your movie."

"I lost my date before the movie started. When I was putting away dinner, she put the movie on and promptly fell asleep. Even though it's getting better every day, it's still strange to think of the girl I used to run and ski with and see the woman who can't stay awake."

"It's been over five years and it's still strange to me, too. She's getting much stronger, though, and the pain seems to be quite a bit less. She'll continue to get better. She's got a strong will and a fighting spirit."

"That she does. I just wish there was something more I could do for her."

"Your being here for her is doing something for her. She lost most of her friends because she didn't have the energy to be around people or do anything, and it's a gift to her to have people around. Up until now, Rachel and Brianna have been the only people who stuck by her. She and Emily have grown close since they've been living together here, and now she has you. That's good medicine." She went into the other room and he resumed his watching and praying over Shelby.

Lord, please show me if there is something I can do to help her. It's so frustrating to have to just wait and hope. Please give me the strength to be the kind of helper she needs. And thank You for giving me a perfect birthday weekend.

He realized as he sat there watching her sleep that he fully understood what people meant when they said, "When you know, you know."

He thought about his two year timeline and knew that he would burn it for her. He didn't need another day to figure out if he wanted to be with her, let alone months.

Chapter 23

Shelby was giddy as she got ready to go to Joe and Emily's wedding. She had spent the week getting extra rest, as planned, and was feeling bored and stir crazy.

Clay had brought her dinner a couple of times and joined her on her short morning walks, but they kept the visits brief. Rachel and the newly-returned Brianna had stayed away too, so she had spent the majority of the week either reading or doing work for the center.

She was feeling better and felt a little silly taking the extra precautions, but she had learned the hard way that if she didn't take enough precautions before big events to prevent crashes, it could take weeks to get back to where she was before.

She was looking forward to getting out of the house, but was especially excited to be spending the day with Clay. Over the previous month she had gotten quite used to spending her evenings with him and she missed him while she was resting up. She had replayed their dance at Rachel and Derek's wedding a thousand times in her head and couldn't wait to do it again at Joe and Emily's. It would be even better because this time she wouldn't have to pretend she wasn't in heaven.

The past month with him had been amazing. She had never been so comfortable with anyone or laughed at so many of the same things with anyone and it seemed they could talk about anything. They had so much in common, with their faith and sports and even with losing the futures they had laid out for themselves. It was nice not to have to try to explain things to him. He understood them because he'd lived them.

She put on the new dress she'd gotten in Traverse City the last time she went for a doctor's appointment and felt like a normal person for the first time in a while. She took care with her makeup and hair and loved having him to look pretty for.

When Clay knocked on the door, her heart leapt, and when she opened it and saw him there in his suit, her stomach did a little dance. He stepped inside and swept her into a hug and twirled her around.

"Wow, look at you! You're even more beautiful than usual."

"I got the dress in Traverse the other day."

He winked at her and gave her a crooked smile. "I hadn't noticed the dress. How are you feeling?"

Shelby blushed. "Hot and bothered now, thanks to you. I'm excited that I get to spend the whole day with you, and you look extra handsome, too."

He laughed along with her. He was still holding her and started swaying with her. "Let's skip the wedding and stay here and dance all night."

She giggled and hid her face in his chest. "Don't tempt me, Mr. Cooper. That sounds like way too much fun."

"It also sounds like way too much temptation. Since I prefer to avoid that than fight it, we'd better get moving."

Chapter 24

C lay felt completely different watching this wedding ceremony than others in the past. He listened to every word spoken and absorbed everything Pastor Ray said about second chances and shared lifetimes. For the first time ever, Clay could imagine himself up at the altar taking the vows with the woman beside him.

His rules about dating and engagement taunted him and he thought again about the action steps involved in trusting God with his future. There was no way he was going to wait for another eleven months to propose to Shelby and then another year to marry her. He was ready to start a life with her and he would trust God with the timing, not his own plans.

When Pastor Ray pronounced Joe and Emily husband and wife, Joe's three-year-old daughter Lily squirmed off her grandmother's lap and ran over to them. As Emily bent down to pick her new daughter up, there was not a dry eye in the place.

The reception was at Bellows Vineyards and Clay was happy to have a bit of a drive there so that Shelby could rest. He tried insisting that she sit quietly with her eyes closed so that she could save her energy and enjoy herself at the reception, but she was having no part of it.

"You've hardly seen me this week and now you're telling me not to talk? Haven't you missed me?"

He laughed. "I'm trying to make sure you have energy left to dance with me. And I've most definitely missed you this week." He kissed her hand and held it as they made their way out to the winery.

May flowers were blooming and the trees covering the hills and valleys as they drove to the other end of Summit County were bursting with new growth. Everywhere they looked was green and it felt like they were surrounded by new life. It seemed fitting to him, as everything in life felt new lately.

The winery wouldn't open for the season until the next weekend, but Pete Bellows was an old friend and had opened it for the wedding as a favor to Joe. The rustic dining room was a perfect setting for a reception, with delicious food and plenty of beautiful views. Clay made a mental note to bring Shelby back when she was feeling up to walking around outside.

They had a great time and he took every opportunity for slow dances. "Who do you suppose I could tip to get them to play only slow songs for the rest of the night? I like having the excuse to hold you close."

She leaned in and whispered in his ear, "You don't ever need an excuse to hold me close."

He felt like a lightening bolt shot through him. He couldn't remember the last time he'd felt so happy, and he pictured his timeline going up in flames.

Chapter 25

Shelby was sitting on the couch working on her computer a few days later when Brianna came in the door with Lily. She was sharing babysitting duties with her parents and Lily's maternal grandparents while Joe and Emily were on their honeymoon, and she and Lily were doing all of their favorite activities together.

"We're having an Auntie Brie and Lily day and she wanted to come and see you."

She whispered to Shelby as Lily walked around, "I think she's looking for Joe and Emily and thinks they're here. Lily, did you show Miss Shelby your pretty fingernails? Show her what we did when we played beauty shop earlier."

Lily walked over and proudly showed her pink nails to Shelby, then climbed up on her lap so she could see them better. When she asked for a book, Brianna handed her one from her bag and Shelby began to read it to her. Since Shelby couldn't play with her on the floor like others for so long, books had become their thing, and Shelby loved reading to her.

When they finished the book, Shelby looked up and saw that Clay had walked quietly into the house and was leaning against the doorway watching them with a big smile on his face.

When Lily saw him, she climbed down and ran over to him excitedly. "Hide seek, Mr. Clay!"

Clay swooped Lily up and spun her around. "Okay, Lily. You go hide!" He put her down and covered his eyes while she hid behind the settee.

Brianna turned to Shelby, smiling. "Mr. Clay is her favorite person to play Hide and Seek with. She was asking if he would be here today."

Shelby's heart was full as she watched him pretend to have a hard time finding her hiding place, then squeal when he 'found' her. Lily giggled as he tickled her and chased her into the library.

Shelby pictured him with his own children and thought about what a great father he was going to make. She could see him playing with his children in his backyard, letting them climb all over him. When she pictured him with the children she would love to have *with* him, reality slammed her like a freight train.

What am I doing? He wants to be a father. He needs *to be a father. I don't even know if I'll be able to have kids.*

It felt like the air had suddenly been sucked out of the room and she felt lightheaded.

It was one thing for him to spend a month having low-key dates, but it was quite another to have the possibility of an entire lifetime of that. While it was true that she was continually feeling better and stronger, she had no guarantee of how much more improvement, if any, she could expect to gain. Asking him to take the chance of foregoing having an active life, and especially having children, was simply too much.

She knew she was holding him back from the life he should have, and she realized she needed to end the best relationship she'd ever had. She scrambled to keep the tears at bay and was relieved that Clay and Brianna were distracted with Lily and weren't looking at her.

I've got to get out of here. She stood on unsteady legs and headed toward the stairs.

"I'm sorry, you guys. I'm not feeling well." She didn't look in their direction or wait for a response from either of them and walked as quickly as she could manage up the stairs. It took all the strength she could muster, but she held it together until she got upstairs. When she got into her room, she burst into tears.

∞∞∞

The next morning she sent Clay a text asking him to come over in the afternoon when her aunt would be at her book club. She then went about preparing for the hardest thing she had ever had to do.

Though she didn't have an athletic body anymore, she still had an athletic mind, and she prepared for the breakup the way she'd prepared for games and meets. She focused on what she would say and practiced her speech over and over in her mind, with several breaks to cry.

She asked God to give her strength to do what she had to do for the man she loved. "Lord, please give me the words and the ability to do this. He needs so much more than I can give and it would be selfish of me to hold onto him and to hold him back. Thank You for the time I've had with him and for showing me what it's like to feel like this. Please help him to see that this is the right thing to do and to move on. Please bring him a wife who can go for hikes and bike rides with him and who can give him as many children as he wants. Please make all of his dreams come true."

Chapter 26

C lay's stomach was in a tight knot as he drove to Shelby's. He couldn't ignore the feeling he had that something was terribly wrong.

When he first walked in the door the day before, she looked happy as she read to Lily. It made him feel warm all over watching them together and picturing her reading to their daughter. It had also served as confirmation to him that he had done the right thing when he had bought an engagement ring a few hours earlier.

She had been laughing watching them play Hide and Seek, and then suddenly she was heading upstairs and not looking back. He and Brianna had shared a look with each other, and Brianna looked as confused as he felt. He thought maybe Shelby had been hit with one of the headaches she sometimes got, but something didn't feel right.

It took all of his willpower to just leave after she went upstairs instead of chasing her down, or at least waiting in case she came back down later. When she didn't answer her phone and gave one-word answers to his texts until she sent one asking him to come over, he got very nervous.

When she opened the door, his fears multiplied. Her eyes were red and it was obvious that she had been crying. When he hugged her, she was tense and moved away quickly.

"Honey, what is it?"

"I'm okay. I just need to talk to you about something." *Uh-oh, this is not good.*

He wondered if she was about to confess some big, deep secret. He knew he could handle whatever it was if that was the case, just like she had when he'd confessed his past failures to her. There was nothing he couldn't or wouldn't understand or forgive her for.

She led him into the parlor and sat stiffly on the end of the couch. He sat in the middle and waited for the ax to fall.

"I need to say something, and it's going to be hard for me to say it, so I need you to listen without interrupting me, okay?"

"Okay." He held his breath as he wondered what could possibly have her so upset.

She looked at her hands as she spoke. "These past weeks have been amazing. *You* have been amazing. It's been the best time of my life."

She took a deep, shaky breath. "But I can't do it anymore. I've been thinking and I've realized that this isn't going to work, that it has to end."

"*What?* Why d—?" He felt like the wind had just been knocked out of him. No hit on the football field could compare to what she had just said.

"Please let me finish." She had tears in her eyes and her voice was strained. "I feel a little bit like a fraud because even though you see that I'm hurting and tired, what you don't realize is that you're seeing the absolute best that I have to offer. The minute we're apart, I usually collapse. I'm even *less* than what you see. I'm way better than I was, but I'm not as well as you think I am and this is not enough for you. You deserve to have a life with someone who can go on hikes and on dates and stay awake past nine o'clock. I can't give you what you need and what you deserve, and I can't hold you back from the life you should be able to have."

"Shelby, what in the world are you talking about? Have I given you the impression that I'm missing out on something?" He was at a loss and had no idea where this was coming from.

"No, not at all. That's part of what makes you so wonderful and what has made our time together so special. You've been great, but I know that I've been your rescue project. You don't need someone to rescue or take care of, though, you need someone who can be your equal, someone you can build a life with. I can't be that right now and I don't know if I ever will. That's why I have to say goodbye to you."

"*Rescue project*–" His chest was so tight he felt like his air supply was getting squeezed out.

He had to strain to push the words out. "Shelby, don't mistake having physical weakness with having to be rescued. Don't take what we have away from us."

"I'm trying to *give* you something, Clay, not take it away. I'm trying to give you a future where you can have a child of your own to play Hide and Seek with and where you don't have to be held back by someone who can't keep up. The sooner we end this, the sooner you can find that."

"Wait, is *that* what this is about? This is about *Hide and Seek?*"

It was starting to make sense now.

"Watching you play with Lily yesterday was the most beautiful thing. Then it was the most excruciating thing, because I don't know if I can give that to you. It's not fair to deny you that."

He couldn't believe what was happening.

"You know that I'm not an impulsive person, Shelby. You know that I'm a planner and that I look far ahead before I leap. I knew what I was getting into when I asked you out and I knew what I was getting into when I started spending as much time as I could with you – and I knew what I was getting into when I fell in love with you. Don't paint me as some kind of victim here. This is what I want – *you* are what I want."

He wished she would say something, but she sat silently crying. He felt his own tears threatening to spill over, too.

"You have been so beaten down by this over the past five years that somehow you've become convinced that you're some kind of consolation prize. You know me – I don't go on pity dates and I don't accept consolation prizes. You are the grand prize, and I'm not giving you up without a fight."

He reached across the space between them and turned her face up to look at him. "If you want to break up with me because you don't love me, I'll wish you well and walk out that door. But if you're doing this because of some misguided idea about what's good for me, I'm not having it. I love you and know you love me."

He gave her a moment to say something and prayed that she wouldn't. She just sat silently and averted her eyes.

"Shelby . . . look me in the eye and tell me you don't love me, and I'll go."

She looked up at him as the tears ran in streams down her cheeks. "Clay, please." Her voice was barely a whisper.

He sighed as he spoke and his tears fell, too. "I knew you couldn't say it. I want to make a life with you, no matter what it holds. If you get better and we can do the things you used to be able to do and we can have kids, great. If not, we'll make a different kind of great life for ourselves and we'll be the best babysitters in Hideaway. I don't care what the future holds, as long as you're in it."

She paused for what seemed like an eternity, barely breathing or moving. "I don't know what to do."

"I do. May I pray for us?"

She nodded as she wiped her eyes. He reached out and pulled

her in under his arm.

He held her close and she rested her head on his chest as he began to pray, "Lord, You are bigger than all of these things. I thank You for every second I've been able to spend with this amazing woman. Please help us both to see what Your will is for us and for this relationship and help both of us to be open to what You have for us. I admit that I have an agenda here – I want You to change Shelby's mind and I want You to give us a long future. But more than that, I want Your will for her life and for mine. Please show us what You want for us, Lord. We both need to hear Your voice and we both want Your will. I pray these things in Jesus' Name. Amen."

She didn't say anything. He looked down and saw that she had fallen asleep. Her head still rested on his chest and he rested his head on hers, taking in what he hoped were not the last moments with her.

Please don't let me lose her, Lord. Show me how to fix this. No. Show me how to trust You to make this right.

Chapter 27

S helby was confused and disoriented; her head was pounding and she was in a daze from a horrible dream. As she became more awake she realized that she was in Clay's arms, and that it was no dream at all.

She remembered the conversation and realized that she must have fallen asleep while he was praying for them. It felt wonderful and horrible at the same time to be held by him. Without thinking, she tightened her grip around his waist, savoring the moment. He did the same and kissed her on the top of her head.

She looked up at him and spoke softly. "I still don't know what to do."

His tone was gentle. "How about if you let me be responsible for me and for what I want out of life, and you be responsible for you, and we give this time?"

She managed a half-smile and nodded.

"What do you want, Shelby?" He looked at her with an intense gaze.

She felt the tears rising up again. "I want you to be happy."

His tears matched hers as he gazed down at her. "I'm happy when I'm with you. We're risk-takers, remember? We both had the futures we'd planned blow up and we both adjusted and formed different lives. If we could do it alone, we can do it together."

She wanted to believe that they could have a future and that it would all turn out well. She knew he was not a man to say things that he didn't mean and she tried to rest in what he'd said.

He stroked her cheek as he spoke softly. "I meant what I said earlier. I'm in love with you and I want to share my life with you. If that means a life of movies on the couch, so be it."

"I love you, too, Clay. Just promise me something, okay?"

He got a teasing glint in his eye. "A couple of hours ago, I would have said I would promise you anything, without knowing what you were going to say. Now I'm older and wiser, so I have to hear what you're asking first."

"I'm serious. I'll give it time, but you promise me that if this all gets to be too much for you, or not enough for you, you'll end it. I won't be your anchor."

"That's easy for me to promise, because that's never going to happen. You'll never be too much *or* not enough for me. You're just right." He squeezed her again.

She loved hearing the words, but it seemed too easy and she was still afraid of being unfair to him. "Thirty days."

"What do you mean?"

"I don't want you to be trapped and you're too good a guy to leave easily, so I want a safety valve. If in thirty days you want out, promise me you'll go. I'm going to ask you again if you want to leave, and I promise I won't hold it against you if you go."

He gave a mock exasperated look and sighed. "Fine. Whatever. I'm not leaving. I'll give you the thirty-day safety valve if you promise to just let things happen and not to talk about breaking up during that time."

"Deal."

He held her close and kissed the top of her head again. She reveled in being in his arms and told herself to treasure every moment of the next thirty days in case it all ended then.

Chapter 28

C lay went over his notes and made sure he had his key questions written down before picking Shelby up for her appointment with Dr. Harden. He had been surprised and relieved when she had finally agreed to let him go with her.

She seemed a little tense as they drove to Traverse City, but made her usual conversation and jokes. "I still don't know how you got me to agree to let you come today."

"I'm really good at sales."

"It makes me a little nervous that you get people to say yes to you for a living." They both laughed and he reached over to hold her hand.

"I'm just glad I got you to say yes to me. Is it still okay for me to go in with you? I promise I'll mostly listen."

"Yes, it's okay, and I told you that you can ask your questions, too. I know you have questions." As she said it, he saw the hint of cloud over her eyes. She hadn't brought up the ridiculous notion of the thirty-day out she'd insisted on two weeks before and he had hoped she'd forgotten about it, but it was clear she hadn't. Part of his goal for the appointment was to show her that he could handle whatever they faced and put her fears to rest.

The doctor was as kind and as competent as Shelby had described, and she seemed pleased with Shelby's progress. She patiently listened to everything Shelby said and answered all of her questions, then turned and addressed him.

"I hope you've been really hearing all that we've been talking about here. One of the hardest things for significant others to understand is why this takes so long, and sometimes they get very frustrated. This is more marathon than sprint, and I hope you realize how well Shelby is doing."

"I do realize that." He looked directly at Shelby as he said, "I knew what the risks were and knew I was signing up for a marathon when I asked her out."

He redirected his gaze to Dr. Harden. "I know that she's doing everything she can. I just wish there were more things *to* do. I see her getting stronger every day and her perseverance inspires me. I'm just looking for how I can help her. I'm not used to patience and giving things time being my action steps."

Shelby reached over and took his hand. "He's been amazingly patient and encouraging, but I brought him today so that he can ask any questions he has and answer any of yours. You have my permission to say anything in front of him, and I don't want you to sugar-coat things."

"Okay, Clay, what are your questions?"

He asked everything on his list, being especially careful to see how Shelby was reacting when he asked about children. He had gotten pretty good at avoiding hidden land mines with her and wanted to extend his record. Dr. Harden was as patient in answering his questions as she had been with Shelby's, and asked for his observations as well.

Shelby was quiet on the way home and Clay hoped he hadn't overstepped.

"How was that for you? Are you upset that I asked some of the things I asked?"

"No. You needed to ask everything you did because you need to be able to make an informed decision about your future."

"*Our* future." He looked at her pointedly. "And I *only* make informed decisions."

"You know what I mean, Clay. You know that just because I can stay awake longer and go on longer walks doesn't mean that everything is fine. I still can't guarantee you that I'll get back to being as active as I was and I can't guarantee—" The words seemed to stick in her throat.

He felt like his frustration was getting to the breaking point and let out a heavy sigh. "Children. I know. You know who else doesn't have a guarantee? Derek and Rachel. And Brianna. And every other person we know who hopes to. Joe and Emily don't have a guarantee that they'll give Lily siblings."

"Now you're mad. This is what I'm trying to prevent."

"I'm not mad at you, I'm mad at the situation. I hate this stupid disease and I hate those doctors who didn't listen to you and do something about it and I hate that I can't fix it for you."

"I hate it too. And I don't want you to end up hating me." He could hear the tears starting again.

"*What*? Hating *you*?"

He was glad to see a parking lot ahead that he could pull into. He pulled into a space away from other cars and turned to fully face her. "What are you talking about?"

"I don't want you to end up hating me if it can't be fixed."

"Shelby, my anger is not *at* you – it's *for* you. I hate that I'm letting you down by not finding a way to make this better."

They both sat silently for a few minutes.

When he couldn't stand it any more, he spoke again. "Shelby, I have never said that you're not trying or that you don't have the right attitude or that you aren't believing enough. I've never said

I can't stand the uncertainty or that I want out. I know you've lost people because of this, but I'm here, and this is where I want to be. When are you going to start believing in me?"

"That's not what—"

"That's what it feels like. I'm trying to do everything I can to show you that I love you and that I'm here for the long haul. Do you really not see it?"

"I do believe in you."

"Then start acting like it."

He was trying to keep his tone calm, but his frustration was seeping through. "You're pushing me away, and I'm tired from fighting it. I'm tired of fighting *you*. You're the one who has the decision to make here. You need to decide if you're going to take me at my word."

When she looked at him, she looked like her heart was broken. "I'm sorry. I never meant to make you feel that way. I just want to protect you."

His heart broke in that moment, too, and he wanted nothing more than to soothe her and make it okay. "And I want to protect you. We're supposed to be protecting each other from the outside world, but you're trying to protect me from *you*. If I protected you from me, I never would have asked you out in the first place."

"What do you mean?"

"When I made bad decisions with women in college, I knew I was doing wrong, but had no idea the depth of regret I would have later. I had no idea that someone like you would ever come along who would make me wish I was a better man. I talked to my dad about you a couple of weeks before I asked you out. I told him there was someone who was off-limits to me for a couple of reasons, one of which was that she was so pure that she was out of my league and I felt unworthy.

"I told him I couldn't be with her, and he told me I should let her be the one to decide if she wanted to be with me instead of taking the decision out of her hands. I thank God every day that he gave me that advice and that I was smart enough to take it. I wish you would take it, too. When I dropped the hint about my past on our first date, I was giving you warning and an out, and you moved forward with me. When I told you everything, you accepted the worst part of me without hesitation. So it seems that we both knew what we were getting into."

"I guess we did. But what are you going to do if this can't be fixed?"

"What *we* are going to do is move on – that's what people like us do. I couldn't fix my knee enough to have my dream career and I moved on. If your body can only be fixed so much, we move on. That's it."

"You make it sound so simple."

"It *is* simple. It isn't easy, but it's simple. When I came back from San Francisco, I thought I had to be a different person and have a completely different life than what I had planned. It took some-one who was like me to get in my face and tell me to be me again and do what I could. I followed your advice and now I have a great life. I even found myself an amazing girlfriend, though she's a bit argumentative and stubborn."

She chuckled and he reached over to hug her. "At least I can still almost make you laugh. I'm not like Jimmy and I'm not going to start blaming you for this or leave you."

He tried again to lighten the mood. "I should have stolen you from him that day at Marvel Point and saved you from that."

She did laugh then. "Yes, you should have. What took you so long with that?"

"I must have hit my head a few too many times." He stroked her cheek and looked earnestly into her eyes. "Can we get back to giving this time and trusting God with it now?"

"Yes." She pulled him close and held him as tightly as she ever had.

"Good. You need to save up some of that stubbornness for the next family game night. Now that I finally have a worthy teammate, I'm ready to keep crushing my parents and the newlyweds."

She giggled as she said, "That really was fun. Your other girlfriends didn't show up ready to win on family game night?"

"My other girlfriends weren't invited."

As they got back on the road and continued the drive to Hideaway, she fell asleep and he prayed that God would somehow make time move more quickly over the next two weeks so that the torturous thirty days could be behind them once and for all.

Chapter 29

Shelby took in the big sand dune. It was so majestic that it always took her breath away when she stood at its base and looked up.

From where they were standing, it didn't look that daunting, but the Sleeping Bear dunes were the best example on earth of things not being as they appear. She used to make the full trek over it to Lake Michigan on the other side at least once per summer, but doing that again was a long way off, at best. Today she planned to go as far as she could and then wait for the others to go to the top and return. She had a book on her phone and planned to do some reading while she waited.

They all started together, and as she slowed, Rachel, Derek, and Brianna separated from her. Clay stayed by her side and acted as if he might stay with her when she stopped about fifteen feet up.

"Clay, I know you want to show them all up by getting to the top first. If you don't get going, there's going to be too much catching up to do, even for you."

"What if I don't want to?"

"You *do* want to. You *always* want to. I'm not talking about that thing we promised not to talk about, but you have to do things I can't do. Remember?"

He put his hands up in surrender. "Okay, I know that look and I'm not going to argue with you. I'll see you in a bit – I'm going to go win for our team."

She was relieved when he kissed her on the cheek and started running up the hill to catch – and pass – the others. She laughed as she watched the others look at each other and shake their heads. They knew from experience that he would win any race to the top.

She pushed herself to walk a few more feet up and sat down facing the two small lakes at its base. The view was beautiful from everywhere on the mass of sand, and she willed herself to appreciate it even though it wasn't from the top. *Someday.*

"Thank You, Lord, for getting me this far. I never could have gotten up here last year at this time – or two months ago, for that matter. Thank You for giving me the healing You have. Please help me to trust You with every part of my future and to put all the uncertainty at Your feet." She knew as she said the word 'uncertainty' that she needed His help to fully embrace it.

The longer she sat there, the more she enjoyed the view. One thing having limitations had taught her was to stop and appreciate things. She took her phone out to take some pictures, but never got around to the book. The view was just too spectacular and was a tangible reminder of how far she had come. Before she knew it, Clay was skidding to a stop next to her.

"Miss me?"

"Yes, I did. Did you go all the way up?"

"Almost. I was following your orders and winning for our team, then remembered that I'm a grown man and I do what I want. I knew I would have more fun down here with you than up there alone, so I ran back down." He grinned at her as he caught his breath and she lost hers.

She couldn't help meeting his grin, as usual. "You gave up winning for me?"

"Didn't you hear my story? I did win. You're my finish line. That smile is my trophy."

He took her phone from her hand and snapped a picture of them together, then one of her where she was sitting. "Photo proof of progress. Look how far you came up here today – that's amazing."

"And you're crazy." *And wonderful. And perfect.*

He moved closer to her and they sat and took in the beauty, arm in arm. He turned to her. "See what I mean? This is way more fun than being up there alone."

Chapter 30

C lay loved the feeling of victory. He turned to Mitch and laughed. "Better luck next time, old man."

"I won't need luck next time if you don't cheat."

"Nice try. Want to go again?"

"Absolutely. Give me the ball." Just as Mitch started dribbling down the court, his phone rang. "You just got lucky. I've got to go."

"How convenient. See you tonight, then."

Clay was looking forward to the fundraiser for the treatment center. They had put in a lot of work and he was feeling confident that it would raise enough money to get the doors open sooner than they had ever dreamed.

He was glad that he'd had it to focus on for the past thirty days, because sitting on the engagement ring he'd purchased thirty-one days before was making him crazy. He was holding to his promise not to talk about the future, even though he'd only agreed to the thirty-day safety valve to get her to stop talking about breaking up. Now that he was only hours away from its official expiration, he had a hard time focusing on anything but getting the ring on her finger and putting any doubt about their future to rest.

He still had nervous energy to burn after taking a shower, so he headed out to Summit Mountain to see if he could start early on any of the setup for the event. Rick and Faith were in the conference room already, and were arguing about getting the boxes of supplies into the room.

When Rick saw Clay, he turned to her with a grin and said, "See? God agrees with me. He even sent Clay to help."

"Uh-oh, what am I walking in on?"

"The lady who lost half of her life due to a back injury was trying to help me unload heavy boxes, and God sent you to stop her."

Clay laughed. "Well, I'm always happy to be used by God."

Faith hugged Clay and laughed. "Wait, you didn't bring Shelby, did you? She's under strict orders not to get here until later."

"No way. She doesn't like it, but she's obeying her boss' orders. She's probably in front of the computer now working on activities for the center, now that there's nothing left to do for the fundraiser."

"Good. She's been a godsend, and I'm so happy that she's been gaining more strength. Since we'll be starting slowly with things, she should be able to do whatever activity programming she needs to without it wearing her out."

Clay was glad to have something physical to do as he and Rick unloaded the rest of the boxes from Rick's Jeep. "Thanks for coming early, Clay. I don't want Faith hurting herself getting ready for this thing, and as you may have noticed, she's a bit stubborn."

"I'm familiar with trying to protect a strong-willed woman from herself." He laughed. "I'm also familiar with losing to her."

"Shelby seems to be doing well. That strong will of hers has brought her far."

"It sure has. She's able to do way more than she was even a couple of months ago, but I still want to protect her. I never want to see her look the way she did that day I drove her home from

Traverse City." He shuddered at the memory of her looking so sick and disoriented.

"Well, if I've learned anything from Faith, it's that these strong-willed women will only tolerate so much protecting. I still try, though, and will fight to the death to keep mine from harm."

"As will I."

"You know Shelby has a special place in my heart. She's part of the reason I have Rachel and Faith in my life and I'm protective of her, especially since she doesn't have a dad anymore." He looked Clay square in the eye. "You're protecting her honor, right?"

"Absolutely."

"Good answer. You have my blessing, for what it's worth."

"That means more than you know."

As they walked in with the last of the boxes, Rachel and Derek pulled up to the building.

"Oh good, more boxes."

The others who had volunteered to help worked together like a symphony, making the room look spectacular. They had accomplished what they set out to, keeping a strict budget and not wasting money that could be used for the center on the party.

Derek had done a masterful job of coming up with ways to repurpose decorations from the recent weddings to make the room look elegant without looking like a wedding reception. His brother's artistic skill never ceased to amaze him, and he prayed that the painting Derek donated for the silent auction would fetch a pretty penny for the center and give his art some exposure. Rachel had finally convinced him to start selling a few paintings in a local gallery, and he was getting some good buzz around town.

∞∞∞

When Clay picked Shelby up for the party, she took his breath away.

"Hello, beautiful." He gave her a lingering hug as he walked in the door. "I wish we were having a movie-on-the-couch date tonight. Let's skip the party."

She laughed, but he thought he saw a flash of sadness on her face.

"Everything okay?"

"Of course. I'm just thinking about the fundraiser."

"Okay. You think about the fundraiser. I'm thinking about how lucky I am to have you on my arm."

She smiled at the compliment, but he couldn't ignore the hint of tension that he saw on her face. He wondered if she was thinking about the thirty-day agreement and wondering if it was all going to end.

She had kept to her promise not to bring it up other than the day of her doctor's appointment, but there were times when he was sure it was on her mind. He was determined to follow the rules of not talking about it, but he wanted to put her mind at ease about his intentions for their future.

He pulled her back into another hug and started swaying with her. "Maybe you can wear that dress when I find a place to take you dancing next weekend, if you're up for it. I'll find a place that plays lots of *slow* music so I can hold you like this all night."

As she rested her head on his chest and swayed along with him, he hoped his hint did the trick.

Chapter 31

S helby looked over at Clay as they drove home from the fundraiser, trying to memorize his face. She had held to her promises to him to not bring up breaking up again and to herself to treasure every moment with him for thirty days, but she was feeling the cloud descending on her.

She wondered if he had forgotten that it was the last day. As he looked over at her and reached for her hand, she forced herself to focus on treasuring the moment.

"I think tonight was a success, don't you?"

She was glad he'd picked a safe topic. "I do. Those testimonies from Faith and her roommate and the other people from the treatment center she was in were amazing. It's so cool that the director from that center came to do the keynote, too. It's obvious than he really believes in the program and in her."

"I was watching the bids on the silent auction items, and we definitely passed the minimum we needed to open the doors."

"I saw that, too. I'm excited that I still have a job after tonight." She hoped that making a joke would mask her tension.

He kissed her hand. "I'm excited for you, too, and proud of you. You're going to be a great asset there. Did you see what Derek's painting sold for?"

"Yes, that was so amazing! I'm really happy for him."

As they got close to her house, she couldn't get away from the thought of what day it was and was desperate to extend the time with him to store up more memories in case everything changed the next day. "Could we stop at the lake for a few minutes before you drop me off?"

His surprised grin melted her heart. "*Absolutely*."

They sat there holding hands and looking out at Lake Michigan. The way the light from the moon and the lighthouse danced across the gentle waves and the sound of the waves lapping against the shore was hypnotic. "It always calms me to sit here and look at that. It puts things into perspective, doesn't it?"

"It does. We're lucky to be able to call a place like this home."

She wanted to stall. She wanted to turn back time to give herself more days. More than that, she wanted to turn back time and take back the promise to give him an out after thirty days. He hadn't shown any signs of changing his mind, but she had to give him the chance to go and had to be ready if he politely backed out of her life.

She thought back to the conversation she'd had with Faith at the fundraiser while they were taking care of the silent auction envelopes.

"Shelby, you tell me when you need to leave, okay? I don't want you crashing."

"I'm okay, I've just got something on my mind. Actually, you might be able to help me. When did you start to believe that you were really getting better?"

Faith had chuckled, but looked sad at the same time. "It was several months in. I felt the improvement in my pain level and had been off all of the meds for months, but every night I begged God to let me feel good the next day as if it was going to vanish or something. Remember, I didn't even tell Rachel I was in the treatment center until I had almost completed the year-long program.

Are you having the same struggles with trusting it?"

"Yes. I feel better every day but I'm terrified that I'll go backwards and end up as bad as I was a year ago. I'm pushing myself more physically, but in other areas I'm holding back."

"With Clay?"

She felt the tears make their way toward her eyes. "I don't want him to be saddled with a sick person."

"I've seen you together, Shelby, and saddled is not the word I would use to describe him. You seem to be the one saddled, but with fear. The fear is completely natural, but I'm here to tell you that believing in the progress you're seeing and feeling is not going to jinx it. There is no spell here, just like there was no spell with me; you're getting better and will probably continue to improve. Even if you don't improve, you've come a long way and won't go backwards." Faith hugged her and held her like someone who understood. "It's okay to hope."

"That's what I've been afraid to do."

"When I finally took the risk to hope that I could have my life back and to trust God with it, everything shifted. That's when I started to really try to make things better with Rachel and when I came up with the plans to start the treatment center I'd been dreaming about. And tonight, I have a better relationship with Rachel than I ever thought we could have and we're on the verge of *opening* the treatment center. And I even got the amazing bonus that I never considered possible with Rick."

She looked her intently in the eye. "You can have happiness, too."

Shelby was finally ready to risk believing – in her recovery and in Clay – if he decided to risk it with her despite the uncertainties that lay ahead. *And now the thirty-day clock that you insisted on is about to strike midnight.*

Clay's gentle voice broke into her thoughts. "Do you want to talk about what's on your mind?"

"Nothing, just watching the waves."

She didn't want to ruin their last night together and forced a reassuring smile in his direction. The look on his face told her he wasn't fooled and knew exactly what she was worried about.

"Truth or dare?"

She laughed nervously. "What are you doing now?"

"Truth or dare?"

She was afraid of what he might ask if she chose truth. "Dare."

"I dare you to look at the time."

"What?"

He gestured toward the clock. "It's past ten o'clock and you're awake and the car didn't turn into a pumpkin. It's midnight some-where and I know you've been thinking about what day tomor-row is all evening. You might as well get your question out so that we can get on with life."

"Clay."

He answered in his most innocent voice. "Yes?"

"It's not funny."

"I agree. I'm just trying to get this over with."

She held her breath and prayed that he hadn't changed his mind as she geared up for the question she was forcing herself to ask.

"Do you want out?"

"No."

As he looked into her eyes, she felt like he was peering into her soul. "That settles it and this conversation is *over*. Let's play again – truth or dare?"

Her relief overwhelmed her and she felt the freedom that only comes with trust. She couldn't help but smile at him.

"Truth."

"Are you ready to take a risk and move forward?" The way he was looking at her made her feel like they could handle anything that came their way.

"Yes." She knew as she said it that she meant it.

It was time to embrace uncertainty and trust God with their future. It was also time to trust that Clay wasn't going to leave.

His smile lit up the car. He pulled her into a hug and they held each other so tightly that she could hardly breathe. His breathing was heavy and she thought she might explode if he didn't kiss her soon.

"You make me so happy. Now will you please agree to go watch the sunset at Marvel Point with me tomorrow? You can have all day to rest up if you need it."

"I would love to." She stifled a yawn, which made both of them laugh.

"Good, now I'd better get you home so that you can start resting up."

After he walked her to her door and gave her a quick good night hug, he turned and made a fast getaway to his car. When she walked in the door, she saw why.

There was a beautiful bouquet of red roses waiting for her in the entryway. Just as she walked over to them and saw no card, a text popped up from him.

"Now that the longest 30 days of my life are finally over, I'm looking forward to us enjoying the next 30 . . . and more."

Chapter 32

Clay tried to settle his breathing as he walked up the steps to her house. He had been waiting for this day for too long and was about to jump out of his skin.

Patience was not his strength, and he wasn't used to having to wait so long to take an action once he had made a decision. Come to think of it, he wasn't used to working so hard in a relationship, either. She was worth the wait and work, though.

When she opened the door, she looked like his relaxed, happy Shelby again. He sent up a quick prayer thanking God for showing her that she could believe him and take a risk on their life together.

"Ready?"

She smiled brightly. "I haven't been on the beach there for a sunset in years. I'm more than ready."

They laughed and talked the whole way out, as if the cloud that had been hanging over them for thirty days had just been blown away. He was relieved and tried to act natural even though he was as nervous as he had ever been. Even though she had agreed to move forward, he hoped he wouldn't scare her off with a proposal so soon.

They found a spot that had a perfect view of the lighthouse and the lake and he spread the blanket out and gestured for her to sit down. She beamed as he sat next to her. "I'm so happy to be here.

It feels so good to have Marvel Point sand in my toes and breathe Marvel Point air again. I'm even happier to be here with you."

"Me too. And I'm happy that the thirty-day safety valve nonsense is over." He smiled at her as he put his arm around her and pulled her close. They sat for a moment, just watching and listening to the waves hitting the shore. He inhaled the warm, fresh air as he readied himself to do what he'd wanted to do since their first date.

"That thirty days just about killed me, you know."

She giggled. "Do you think you're being ever so slightly dramatic?"

"Not at all. Before you started talking crazy and putting thirty-day valves on me, I bought something and it's been burning a hole in my pocket ever since."

She looked confused and seemed to have no idea what he was getting at.

"Shelby, I told you I loved you and wanted to make a life with you. Did you really think I would say something like that without being ready to back it up?"

As he spoke, he rose enough to kneel on his good knee.

Her eyes grew wide and she looked down at the ring he was holding in his hand.

"I dare you to put this ring on your finger and marry me."

Her smile – the real, bright, carefree Shelby smile – grew across her face as it all registered for her. "Oh my gosh. Yes, I'll take that dare!"

He put the ring on her finger before she could change her mind and kissed her hand, then cupped her face with his hands.

"I love you, Shelby, and I can't wait to spend forever with you."

He leaned in slowly and could barely breathe by the time his lips finally touched hers. Her lips were as soft and perfect as he had imagined, and her kiss was well worth the wait.

"What took you so long?" She was out of breath and grinning as she asked.

"I promised God that the next woman I kissed would be my fiancée. It was easy to keep that promise until you came along. You have no idea what you do to a man."

She kissed him again and pulled him back down beside her. "And you have no idea what you do to a woman. My lips have been very jealous of all the attention my hand has been getting."

"I promise I'll make up for it." He leaned in to start making it up to her lips.

She broke into a giggle as she gave him a mocking look. "But, Clay, what about your timeline? Aren't you violating your sacred oath to yourself or something?"

"I knew when I left your house after our first date that I was going to violate my one-year-til-engagement timeline for you."

Her eyes twinkled. "I dare you to violate the one-year-til-wedding one, too."

"I'll definitely take that dare. Now that I've finally won the grand prize, I'm a big fan of short engagements. I'm ready for any date you want – please make it soon."

Dear Reader,

Hopefully if you've read this far, you enjoyed the book! I know you're busy and have other things (and books!) clamoring for your time and attention, and I hope this story brought a little brightness into your day.

Clay and Shelby will continue to pop up in smaller roles in other books in the series and you can see their story progress along in the background while other residents of Summit County take center stage.

If you would like to leave a review on Amazon so that other readers can be introduced to this book, I would be so grateful. If having to leave a full review is just too much (I get it - they take precious time that could be spent reading!), but you'd like to leave a rating on Goodreads, you can do that, too!

See you in Summit County,

Katherine

Summit County Series, Book 5

Repairing Hearts in Summit County

Can two people who have been burned badly let love in?

Mitch led a quiet life filled with running his business, being active in his community, and helping his nephew adjust to life after combat. He had returned to Hideaway after suffering his own wounds in love and war and set about creating a very different life from the one he'd planned for himself.

Bella came to Hideaway after the cold life she had chosen in an attempt to please her family was exposed for what it was by her cheating husband. When her world imploded and she had nowhere to turn, she left it all behind and started a new life on her terms.

Neither was looking for any kind of romance, especially after meeting each other at their worst moments, but once they stopped fighting their feelings – and each other – they knew life would not be the same again.

Available on Amazon in Kindle and Paperback formats!

About the Author

Katherine Karrol is both a fan and an author of lighthearted, sweet, clean Christian romance stories. Because she does not possess the ability or desire to put a good book down and generally reads them in one sitting, she writes books that can be read in the same way.

Her books are meant to entertain and even possibly inspire the reader to take chances, trust God, and laugh at life. The people she interacts with in her professional life have absolutely no idea that she writes these books, so by reading this, you agree to keep her secret.

If you would like to contact her to share your favorite character or share who you were picturing as you were reading, you can follow her on Goodreads, Bookbub, Facebook, Twitter, and Instagram, or email her at KatherineKarrol@gmail.com.

About the Summit County Series

The Summit County Series is a group of standalone books that can be read individually, but those who read all of them in order will get a little extra something out of them as they see the characters and stories they've read about previously continue and will get glimpses of characters that may be featured in future books. It is set in a small county in Northern Michigan, where everyone knows everyone else, so the same characters and places make cameos and sometimes show up in significant roles in multiple books.

This series is near and dear to the author's heart because she spends as much time as possible in places that look an awful lot like the places in Summit County. She is certain that the people who know her and/or live in the area that inspired Summit County will think characters and situations are based on them or their neighbors (or even on her) and she assures them that they are not. The characters and stories are merely figments of her overly active imagination. Well, except for Jesus. He's totally real.

The books are all available on Amazon in paperback and Kindle formats.

Books in the Summit County Series

Second Chance in Summit County

Trusting Again in Summit County

New Beginnings in Summit County

Taking Risk in Summit County

Repairing Hearts in Summit County

Returning Home in Summit County

Made in the USA
Monee, IL
13 August 2020

38195941R10094